ACKNOWLEDGEMENTS

Procrastination is an art form I've perfected, self-doubt is a nightmare that literally keeps me awake at night, and technology is the bane of my existence. So *no*, I definitely could not have done this on my own.

To Kimberly, thank you for donating so much of your time to editing my books. If I actually make money from this, I swear I'll pay you! Thank's for being my cheerleader when I needed one, and for being the best friend a girl could have.

To everyone in the 20BooksTo50K group, thank you for teaching me everything I know about self publishing. Every "The End" post, and every success story gave me the motivation to keep going when things got tough.

To my fabulous beta team- Amber, Jasmin, Lisa, Rachelle, Reiana, Sadie, Sandra, and Taylor. Thanks for giving a newbie author like me a chance, and for devoting so much of your time to helping me through this process. You are all amazing!

And to my husband, thank you for believing in me, and for never letting me give up on my dream of becoming an author. And thanks for bragging to everyone you meet that your wife is an author (even though it defeats the whole purpose of me using a pen name). I love you.

CONTENT WARNING

This book contains the following content which might be troubling to some readers: graphic sex, graphic violence, graphic blood depictions, murder, vomiting, forced proximity, captivity, mention of drug use, mention of terminal illness (off page, historical context), mention of suicide (off page, historical context), cliffhanger.

THE DARKEST SONG

AMY ATLEY

Cover Artist: Andrea @ CReya-tive Book Cover Design

CONTENTS

Part One

Part Two

PART ONE

Kissed By Darkness

Could you love someone who held you captive? Someone who took away your free will, and delighted in the death of someone you loved?

No.

At least that's what I used to think...

CHAPTER 1

A cold wind blew past me, and I shivered, mentally cursing myself for the millionth time for wearing a sundress. Jeans and a hoodie would've been the smarter choice, but I always got more tips when I wore a dress.

I was in my usual spot, by the fountain at the edge of the park, where tourists always stopped to take pictures. Restaurants and bars lined the opposite side of the street, and crowds of people milled about, waiting for the night to begin.

I was playing my violin, as I did almost every night, and was currently in the middle of a Star Wars medley, where I started with "Binary Sunset," flowed into "The Imperial March," and ended with "Duel Of The Fates." It was one of my most popular songs, and a large crowd had gathered to listen.

I drew my bow across the strings in the final, dramatic note, and the crowd erupted into cheers. People began tossing dollars into the violin case at my feet, and I smiled in thanks, and immediately began to play again.

With the excitement of Star Wars over, the crowd quickly dispersed, and as I glanced down at the pile of money in my case, my smile grew wider. *I needed this.* Even working full time at the diner and playing my violin every night, I was still behind on rent. But it looked like my luck was finally changing.

I glanced down at the pile of cash again, then looked up and caught the eye of a guy standing at the edge of the street. *Shit.*

I quickly looked away, but it was too late, he was already coming towards me. I continued to play, pretending I didn't notice him. He was accompanied by three other guys, and they were all obviously drunk.

"Hey!" he called as he walked up to me. I kept my face turned away, pretending to concentrate on my music.

"Hey," he said again, as his group came to a stop right in front of me. They were standing so close I could smell the alcohol on them. No longer able to ignore him, I smiled tightly and continued to play.

"You're real good," he said loudly. "Real *hot* too."

I took a step back, and he reached out and grabbed the skirt of my dress. I yanked away, my bow screeching as it yanked across the strings as I abruptly stopped mid-song.

"Don't touch me!" I snapped, gripping my bow tightly in my fist. I knew it would break if I struck him with it, but with my mace tucked away in my backpack on the ground, it was the only weapon I had.

He straightened and glared at me, then his friend slapped him on the shoulder and said, "Come on man, let's go."

They turned and started walking away, and when I heard one of them call me a stuck-up bitch I had to clench my jaw to stay silent. My heart was pounding with anger, and I had to take several deep breaths to calm myself before I could play again.

It figures, just when I was finally having a good night, a bunch of assholes would have to come along and ruin it. I wanted to pack it in and go home, but I'd never cut a Friday night short. Weekends were my most profitable nights, and I couldn't play tomorrow since I was going home to see Allie, so I swallowed my anger and kept playing.

But my night was already ruined. My emotions always flowed through my music, and my foul mood was obvious to the tourists passing by. I played for another hour before someone else stopped to tip me, and just as the woman was reaching into her purse it started to rain.

She shrieked and ran for cover, forgetting all about my tip. I swore and hurried to pack up, shoving my tips into my backpack and zipping up my violin. I shoved my arms through the straps of my backpack, grabbed my violin, and started walking home, but I only made it a few steps before it really started to pour.

I clutched my violin to my chest and broke into a jog. It was only four blocks to my apartment, but by the time I got to my street the rain was coming down so hard I could hardly see where I was going.

I'd just made it to the front steps of my building when someone grabbed me from behind and yanked me backwards. I screamed as I was spun around and thrown to the ground. I hit the street face first, my chin slamming into the wet pavement. The impact stunned me, and for a moment I couldn't move, or even breathe. I lay paralyzed as my assailant yanked my backpack off me, twisting my arms back painfully. Then he let go.

I scrambled to my feet and spun around to face him, but he was gone. I looked around frantically, barely able to see through the pouring rain, but couldn't see him anywhere. I saw my backpack on the ground a few feet away, so I grabbed it and ran up the steps into my building.

I bolted up the four flights of stairs to my apartment and fumbled to get the keys out of my backpack. I jammed them into the lock, looking over my shoulder in case I was being followed, and when I finally got the door open, I rushed inside and quickly slammed it shut and locked it.

Sobbing, I wiped my face with my hands then froze when I saw blood on them. I rushed to the bathroom to look in the mirror. My wet hair was plastered to my head and half of my face was covered in blood. I turned on the sink and frantically splashed water on my face, washing away enough blood to reveal that my chin and right cheek were scraped raw.

With shaking hands I wet a washcloth and tried to clean myself. Tears streamed down my face as I washed. *It should hurt more.* I realized I was probably in shock. *I should call the police.*

I went back to my backpack to get my phone, and that's when I realized I didn't have my violin. I dropped my backpack and ran to the window, but was unable to see through the rain. *Should I go down to look for it? What if my attacker was still out there? The security door was broken, he could be in the building!*

I stumbled to my backpack once more, got out my phone and called the police. They arrived 40 minutes later.

They came up to my apartment to question me, then went back down to look for my violin. But it was gone. They offered to give me a ride to the hospital to have my face looked at, but I declined. I didn't have insurance and a hospital bill was the last thing I needed right now. After they left, I crawled into bed and cried myself to sleep.

CHAPTER 2

I jerked awake to the sound of my phone ringing, wincing as pain shot through my head. I groaned and squeezed my eyes shut, even as I fumbled for my phone on my bedside table.

"Hello?" I groaned as I brought the phone to my ear.

"Hey, it's me," Allie said on the other end. Of course it was Allie. My sister was the only one who ever called me.

"Hey," I said, trying to sound wide awake.

"I'm just calling to make sure you're still coming today."

Shit. "Yeah, I'm still coming." *Only because I couldn't think of another excuse to put her off.*

"Because you said that last time."

"I'm coming, Allie." For a moment, there was nothing but silence on the other end.

"I know this isn't easy for you-"

"I said I'm coming," I said, cutting her off.

Allie was silent for a moment before responding. "Okay. I'll see you at four."

I hung up without saying goodbye and immediately felt guilty. I hated that our relationship had become so strained. It was entirely my fault, but I didn't know how to change things.

I got up to make a cup of coffee, and groaned when I saw I was down to my last scoop. I could go without a lot of things, but coffee wasn't one of them. I upended the bag to get every last bit out and flicked the pot on. Then I went over to my backpack to count last night's tips.

I dug the money out of my backpack, and saw my mace at the bottom of the bag. *A lot of good that did me.* I usually walked home with it clutched in my hand, but I'd been in such a hurry because of the rain, I'd forgotten all about it.

I counted out my tips and had forty seven dollars. *Fuck.* I should've made twice that much on a Friday night, but at least it was enough to buy food. I'd been surviving on ramen all week and desperately needed something healthy.

I drank my coffee and got ready for the day, then headed out to buy groceries. When I opened my apartment door and saw the pink slip taped to it, I groaned. I was only three days late, but my landlord didn't mess around. I pulled the paper down and stuffed it into my pocket before locking the door and heading downstairs.

I skirted past the homeless guy sleeping in the lobby, and went outside. I spent a couple minutes looking for my violin, hoping the police missed it in the rain, but of course it was gone. Anything of value that got left outside in this neighborhood was immediately stolen.

I felt heartbroken. Losing my violin was like losing part of myself. The *best* part. The only part worth having.

It was all I could do not to cry as I walked the half mile to the grocery store. When I got there, I carefully selected the most necessary items that I could cover with my meager funds. But I miscalculated, and when I got to the checkout I didn't have enough and had to put some things back. There was a line of people behind me and I was mortified.

The cashier looked at me with sympathy. "It's alright hun, it happens all the time." Her kindness only made me feel worse, and I blinked as my eyes welled up.

By the time I got back home, I was sweaty and miserable. I stopped in the lobby to get my mail, then started trudging up the stairs. I made it to the third floor before one of my bags ripped and my groceries went tumbling down the stairs, and for the third time that day I blinked at the tears in my eyes.

I gathered it all up and continued up to my apartment. After putting my groceries away, I looked through my mail, but it was just junk and my electric bill. I ripped open the envelope and saw the pink paper inside, and knew it was a disconnect notice. Pink papers are always bad news.

I closed my eyes, feeling utterly defeated. Then I opened them and shoved away from the counter. I didn't have time for self pity, I had a bus to catch.

It was a three hour bus ride back to Mooresville. Being the small town that it was, there wasn't even a proper bus station. They just dropped people off in front of the post office. My bus arrived fifteen minutes early, but Allie was already there waiting. She was parked right in front, in mom's old white Chevy Impala.

I stepped down off the bus, my feet barely touching the ground before the doors closed behind me. I was the only person getting off here.

Allie waved at me, smiling, but then her expression changed to one of horror, making me realize I hadn't told her about my attack. *Shit.* It was a fifteen minute drive to the house, and I spent the first ten reassuring her I was fine.

She had a white-knuckle grip on the steering wheel as she berated me for my life choices. "You need to move! Your neighborhood is the worst! I don't understand why you stay there!"

"It's all I can afford," I reminded her.

"You could have stayed here with me."

I turned my head to look out the window, and we drove the rest of the way in silence.

A few minutes later, I was standing in the drive, staring at the house. Allie went inside, leaving me alone in the driveway. I wanted to get back in the car and drive away. Telling myself this was the last time I'd ever have to be here, I finally mustered the strength to go inside.

It was exactly the same. Allie hadn't changed anything. I walked through the downstairs of the house, seeing my mom everywhere.

In the living room her soft fleece throw blanket was still draped over the back of the sofa, and her books were stacked haphazardly all over the place. In the kitchen, her coffee mug was sitting on the counter. I walked over and picked it up, running my thumb over the small chip on the rim. It was pink with a rainbow on one side, and *I love you* on the other. Allie had painted it as a mother's day gift when we were little, and mom had used it every day.

Allie walked into the room and I gave her a weak smile. "You've been using mom's mug."

"I couldn't let fine art like that grow dust in the cupboard," she said with a laugh. I smiled and set the cup down. "I'm glad you're here," she said softly.

I just nodded, letting my eyes wander around the room before landing on Allie. My sister was like a *new and improved* version of myself. My long hair wasn't quite blonde, wasn't quite brown, and had small, wispy pieces around my face that stuck out awkwardly when it was damp out. Allie's was the color of moonlight, and as smooth as silk. My hazel eyes looked plain old brown most of the time, hers were a striking green. I was 5'9," just tall enough that my jeans were always a little too short. She was a perfect 5'6." I was angry and bitter about the hand I'd been dealt. She was kind and optimistic. Everything about her was soft and feminine. Just like mom. They were so much alike that I had a hard time being around Allie now.

"Mr. Brooks left some papers for us to sign," she said, interrupting my thoughts. She pulled out a chair and sat down at the table. "I think we should have a lawyer look them over first. What do you think?"

I sighed heavily and sat in the chair across from her. "We can't afford a lawyer. And we can't afford to keep the house."

"But his offer is insultingly low!"

I didn't doubt it, but it was the only offer we'd get. "No one else is gonna buy this house, Allie. This is the middle of nowhere. The only reason Brooks made an offer is because his place is next door and he wants to expand his pasture. His offer is crap, but it's him or the bank. And if the bank takes it, we won't get anything."

"It's not fair," she whispered, staring at the table. "What am I going to do?"

"You can come stay with me."

She shot me a look that told me exactly what she thought of that idea, and I couldn't blame her. After all, I'd just been attacked in front of my building.

"With both our incomes we could afford a better apartment," I told her.

She shook her head. "Why can't you move back here? I could get you a job at the office?" She looked at me hopefully, but we both knew that would never happen.

We spent the rest of the evening in the kitchen, talking for hours about absolutely nothing. Well, Allie talked. I mostly listened. She filled me in on all the town gossip I'd missed out on over the last year.

"Mrs. Perkins died and her son moved back home and now he's renovating the house, making all kinds of changes. And he's still single, if you can believe it. Amber had her baby. It's a girl. They named her Grace. Dan still asks about you every time I run into him." Allie chattered on and I just sat there nodding at the appropriate moments.

When we got hungry Allie made grilled cheese sandwiches with dill pickles in them, just like mom used to make. For a while, things almost seemed normal. Then she mentioned Mr. Brooks again and the mood soured.

"He comes by almost every day," she told me. "I keep the curtains closed and pretend I'm not home, but the car is right there in the driveway, so he knows I'm just avoiding him." She frowned. "Sometimes I think It would be smarter to just burn the place down and collect the insurance."

I laughed, but had an uneasy feeling that she wasn't joking.

"Are you going to read the papers?" she asked.

"I'm starting to get a headache," I told her as I stood. "I'm going to bed."

"Okay. The papers are on dad's desk."

I nodded and walked out of the kitchen. I went into my dad's office, grabbed the folder off the desk, and walked out. I didn't want to spend a second longer than necessary in that room. If I had my way, it would have been cleared out last year after he died. But Allie wouldn't let me touch it. So I left and never came home until today.

I went upstairs, stopping by my room long enough to toss the folder on the bed before heading to the bathroom for a long hot shower. I wasn't lying when I told Allie I had a headache, and my face was killing me. I stood in the shower until the hot water ran out, then I wrapped a towel around myself and headed back down the hall to my room.

Just like the rest of the house, my bedroom was exactly the same. It was like I was just coming home from a weekend away. Half of my clothes were still in the dresser, so I put on an old t-shirt and a pair of blue plaid pajama pants, then I grabbed the folder of papers and scooted back against my headboard to read.

I got halfway through the first page before I tossed the folder on the floor in disgust. It *was* an insulting offer. I wanted to tear it up and throw it in Brooks' face. After paying off the bank, there'd be nothing left over for Allie and I.

I felt anger welling up inside of me. Allie was right, this wasn't fair. It wasn't fair that mom got sick. It wasn't fair that we had to say goodbye to all our friends and move to the middle of nowhere because the doctor thought clean country air might help. And it wasn't fair that mom died anyway. Then dad decided he couldn't live with his grief and took the easy way out. He abandoned us when we needed him most. *Damn him.*

I closed my eyes and lay my head back against the headboard. All of mom's life insurance money had been used to pay off her medical bills. Dad's policy was declared void because of his suicide. And what small amount Allie and I made wasn't enough to pay the mortgage on this place. So now we were behind on our payments, the bank was threatening to foreclose, and our only option was to sell to Brooks.

I wanted to sell immediately after dad killed himself, but Allie wanted to stay. The house was all she had left of our parents, and she couldn't bear to leave. So I left instead. It had been a selfish thing to do; I knew that. But like Allie couldn't bear to leave, I couldn't bear to stay. I couldn't bear to be reminded every day of my parents. Being back here now was suffocating.

I opened my eyes. *I had to get out of that house.*

CHAPTER 3

I crept from my room, not wanting Allie to hear me. I didn't want to talk anymore. I needed to be alone. I snuck down the hall, coming to a stop in front of my parent's room. I reached for the doorknob and paused. I hadn't been in their room since we buried my mother. I took a deep breath and opened the door.

I quickly glanced around and saw mom's violin case by the dresser, where she always left it. I grabbed it and got out of there as fast as I could. In my haste, I couldn't remember if I even shut the door behind me. I felt shaky as I rushed down the stairs. I heard Allie in the kitchen, so I snuck out the front door. I didn't even realize I was barefoot until I stepped onto the gravel driveway. I went around to the back of the house and started across the lawn. I passed mom's flower garden, and by the light of the moon I could see that Allie had cared for it meticulously. After a large expanse of mowed lawn, our property opened up to an eight acre field, surrounded by state forest on two sides, and Brooks' property on the third.

I walked out into the middle of the field, far enough from the house that I knew Allie wouldn't hear me, then I took mom's violin out of its case and began to play.

Music had always been the only way I could express my-self, and what I played that night reflected all the anger and heartache that had consumed my life for the last few years.

I stood in the tall grass and played my heart out. I played for hours, as the moon moved across the sky. Sometimes tears would run down my face, but I didn't bother to wipe them away. When I finally reached the point when I could play no more, I let my arms fall to my sides, gripping the violin in one hand and the bow in the other.

"I can't do this anymore," I whispered. "Please," I begged, searching the night sky. "I need this to be over. I need-" I broke off, not knowing what to say.

I don't know how long I continued to stand there, searching the sky for answers. Eventually, I put mom's violin in its case and walked back to the house.

I slept late the next day, and when I finally came down to the kitchen Allie was at the table with her laptop open in front of her.

She raised her eyebrows at me. "Morning sunshine."

I looked at the clock on the stove. It was eleven. "Morn-ing," I mumbled, shuffling across the room to the coffeepot. I grabbed a mug out of the cupboard and poured myself a cup, adding a substantial amount of creamer, then leaned back against the counter and took a long sip. I was physically and emotionally drained from my late-night concert under the stars.

"So I've been thinking about this all night," Allie began, closing her laptop. "If you move back here for *one* year-" She saw the look on my face and held up a hand. "Hear me out, okay?" I groaned and sat down. "If you move back here for *one* year, we could combine our incomes to help get us caught up on the mortgage. Then I can refinance the house in my name alone, and you could go to Juilliard!"

"Juilliard," I repeated, taken aback.

She nodded. "Yeah, you could-"

"I'm not going to Juilliard," I interrupted, as I set my mug down on the table.

"But you have your scholarship, so-"

"That was years ago, Allie," I said incredulously. "It wasn't an open-ended, lifetime offer." I was getting angry now. *Why did she have to bring up Juilliard?* "Do you think they've been saving a spot for me all this time? Besides, I'm too old now."

"I followed you outside last night," she said, her voice softening. "I listened for a while. You sounded like mom."

I stood up angrily. "I signed the papers. I suggest you do the same."

I took mom's violin with me when I left. Allie stared at it when I came out of the house, but she didn't say a word. We rode to the bus station in silence, but when I opened the door to get out of the car, she finally spoke.

"I love you, Sarah."

I looked at her. "I love you too Allie." I swallowed at the lump in my throat. "I'm sorry that I can't be the person you need me to be. It's just too hard. Sometimes I think I'm as bad as dad."

"It's okay." She touched my arm. "It's just a house right? It's just a building. I'll be fine." She smiled at me reassuringly.

She was just like mom. So selfless. I should stay. I should move back home and find some way to save the damn house. Instead, I got out of the car, not knowing it was the last time I'd ever see her.

I t was dark when I got off the bus, so I took a cab to my apartment. I paid the driver and made sure I had my mace in hand before I rushed up the steps to get inside. I was terrified that my attacker might be lurking around.

Once inside, I ran upstairs, taking the steps two-by-two. The lights were out on the third floor landing, and I panicked as I raced through the darkness, almost sobbing with relief when I approached the fourth floor and saw the lights were all on. I dug my keys out of my pocket as I hurried down the hall.

When I got to my door, I unlocked it and pushed it open, relieved to have made it safely home. I stepped into my apartment and was suddenly slammed into from behind.

I didn't even have time to cry out. My assailant grabbed me from behind, with one arm around my rib cage, pulling me back against him. His other hand was clamped tight over my mouth, silencing me. I tried to struggle, but he was too strong. I kicked my feet back into his legs, but it didn't phase him. I tried to bite his hand, but he tightened his grip on my face and yanked my head to the side. I felt a searing pain on the side of my neck, and then my world went dark.

CHAPTER 4

I woke to the phone ringing. I felt a moment's confusion, not knowing where I was, and then the pain hit me. It felt like a thousand knives stabbing me all over my body. I wanted to scream from the agony of it, but I was paralyzed. So I just lay there, praying for the feeling to pass. My phone stopped ringing and for a moment I felt the tiniest relief. Then it rang again, the sound like a hammer to my head.

A coldness swept over me, and I began to shake uncontrollably. The shaking intensified the pain, and a whimper escaped me. Tears rolled from the corner of my eyes down into my hair. The phone stopped ringing, but this time the pain did not subside.

A sharp spasm went through me, causing my body to jerk against my will. Bile rose in my throat, and I rolled onto my side, the fear of choking on my vomit giving me the strength to move. I tried to clench my jaw shut, but the chills shaking me made it impossible. I stretched my arm out and gripped the edge of the mattress. Another spasm hit me, and my knees jerked up towards my chest, my body curling into a fetal position.

Nausea hit me again, stronger this time, and I managed to pull myself towards the edge of the bed, just far enough to hang my head over the side before passing out again.

A text alert woke me the second time, and the first thing I noticed was that the pain was gone. In fact, all feeling was gone. My body felt numb and heavy. I cracked open my eyes and squinted towards the window, trying to gage the time by the tiny sliver of sunlight that crept in over the top of my curtains.

Yes, those were my curtains. I was in my own bed, though I had no memory of how I came to be in this condition. Had I been drugged? My tongue felt thick and stiff in my mouth.

I struggled to sit up and swing my legs over the side of the bed. I sat there a moment, clinging to the edge of the mattress. Then another text alert sounded, drawing my attention to my backpack on the floor by the door. I knew there was no way I could make it across the room in my current condition, so I just sat there, staring at it.

What happened to me? I started to lay back down, but paused when I noticed a large dark spot on the bed. I squinted at it in the semi-darkness for a moment, then reached for the lamp beside my bed.

My arm felt heavy, making me clumsy, and I knocked the lamp over when I turned it on. Light flared into the room, and the first thing I noticed was the dried blood on the back of my hand.

My eyes darted back at the bed, and I saw that the dark spot was also dried blood, right where my head had been. I jumped up from the bed, swaying unsteadily as I looked around. I looked down at myself and saw blood on the front of my shirt.

I tried to run to the bathroom but my numb legs caused me to stumble and fall. I crawled the rest of the way and gripped the edge of the sink to pull myself up. When I saw my reflection in the mirror, I cried out.

My hair was a tangled mess, and my cheek and neck were crusted with dried blood. The collar of my shirt was torn, exposing one blood smeared shoulder. I looked down at my body, frantically searching for injuries. My jeans were still fastened, and I paused for a moment, thankful to know I hadn't been raped.

I turned on the faucet and began splashing water all over my face and neck, and when I lifted my head to look in the mirror I froze. The blood had washed away to reveal smooth, flawless skin. My injuries from being thrown to the pavement were completely healed.

I slowly lifted a shaking hand to touch my chin. I stared at my reflection in disbelief. Then I noticed a small cut at the base of my neck. I leaned closer to the mirror to get a better look. It was not a cut; it was two small holes.

I stared at them, as if in a trance, until my phone rang again. My body jerked, and I grabbed the edge of the sink to stop myself from collapsing. I started to cry, great heaving sobs bursting from my chest. I continued to stare in the mirror as I cried, unable to look away from the marks on my neck. After a moment my phone's ringing pierced through my hysteria, and

I stumbled out of the bathroom, desperate to answer before they hung up.

"Help!" I tried to yell, but the word came out a hoarse whisper. I lurched across the room, collapsing onto the floor beside my backpack just as my phone stopped ringing. I dug through my backpack and yanked my phone out just as it rang again.

I saw my sister's number and answered with a sob. "Allie!"

"Sarah!" she exclaimed. "What's wrong? Are you okay?"

For a moment, all I could do was cry into the phone.

"What's wrong?" she kept repeating, yelling at me.

"I don't know," I finally said between sobs. "I-" I stopped, not knowing how to explain what had happened. With one hand I wiped at the tears on my face.

"Sarah! What's wrong?" Allie shouted again. "Where are you?"

"I'm home," I said. Then, remembering, I raised a hand to my neck and gently touched the two small holes. I took a deep breath and tried to calm myself. "Something's happened." I struggled to stand up.

"What happened? I don't understand."

I looked around my apartment. Other than the bloodstain on my bed, there was nothing out of place.

"Sarah?" Allie was no longer shouting, but she still sounded concerned. "What's going on? I've been trying to reach you all day."

"I don't know." My face was completely healed. How was I supposed to explain that? "I was sick," I said, "but then-" My words trailed off as I slowly walked over towards the wall of blackout curtains covering my two windows.

"Sick? You sounded hysterical when you answered the phone."

"No, I'm okay now." I raised a shaky hand, grabbed the edge of the curtain, and yanked it open. No one was lurking behind them, both windows were shut tight.

It was dark out. *How long had I been sleeping?* I ran my free hand over my cheek and chin, astonished by the smoothness, when only yesterday it had been scabbing over.

"Hello?" Allie said loudly, getting my attention. "Are you still there?"

"Yeah." I turned away from the window.

"You either tell me what's going on, or I'm getting in the car right now and coming over."

"No!" I said, with more force than intended. I didn't know what was going on, but I knew I didn't want my sister involved. "I'm fine." I scrambled to think of something believable to say. "I was sleeping when you called, and I was having a nightmare. It just took me a minute to snap out of it I guess."

"A nightmare." I could hear the disbelief in her voice.

"I'm sorry I worried you. I guess I'm still shook up from getting attacked."

Allie's tone immediately changed. "Of course you are," she said soothingly. "You should have stayed here a few more days."

"Yeah, but I'm okay now. I'll call you later."

"Okay. You can call anytime. I'll be awake."

"Thanks. Bye." I hung up and looked at the time on my phone. It was quarter to eight. I'd been out for almost twenty-four hours. I let the phone drop to the floor and walked back to the bathroom.

I looked in the mirror, my eyes going straight to the holes on my neck. As I stared at them, images began to flash through my mind. *The lights had been out on the third floor. I turned my key in the lock. I made it inside. Someone grabbed me from behind. There was a sharp pain in my neck. Then nothing.* I shook my head. *No, not nothing. There was pain in my neck, but something else as well. I felt his mouth on my skin. The room was spinning. Darkness.*

I pressed a hand against my stomach, remembering the feeling. Sharp pain twisted in my stomach, and I gasped and fell back against the wall. The pain came again, and some primal part of me recognized it for what it was. *Hunger.*

I stumbled out of the bathroom and rushed over to the fridge. I yanked open the door with such force that the condiments on the door went flying to the floor. My eyes quickly spotted the ground beef, and I grabbed it, ripped the plastic open, and shoved my face directly into the raw meat. I ate like an animal, choking down half the plastic wrap in the process.

I devoured a pound of meat in a matter of seconds, then I tilted the styrofoam tray into my mouth and drank the blood that had pooled at the bottom. When I had finished every drop, I tossed the tray to the floor and licked at the blood running down the side of my arm. Then I let my arm fall to my side, and the realization of what I'd done sank in.

I swallowed hard, feeling nauseous, then rushed to the bathroom and emptied the contents of my stomach into the toilet. I knelt there, gasping between heaves. *God, what was happening to me?* I lay down in front of the toilet and closed my eyes.

When I opened my eyes again, I couldn't tell if I'd been sleeping, or just laying there with my eyes closed. I stood up and looked in the mirror. For a moment I just stared at the two holes on my neck. Then I flicked off the light and walked out of the bathroom.

I looked around my apartment. My curtains were open, and I could see that it was still dark out. I saw the bloodstains on my bed. The refrigerator door was still open, and condiment jars were all over the place. I walked over to where my backpack and phone still lay on the floor, and picked up my phone to check the time. It was just past midnight. I'd been on the bathroom floor for four hours.

I set my phone down on the counter and started picking up the condiments. When my work was done, I closed the refrigerator door and leaned back against it. *What next?* My mind felt clouded, like I was dreaming.

"Focus," I said aloud. "You can figure this out." I pushed away from the fridge and started pacing. I rubbed my face, still in disbelief that my wounds had disappeared. I tried to think, but one word kept disrupting my thoughts. *Vampire.*

It was impossible. Vampires weren't real. But every time I looked at the holes in my neck, that's what I thought of. I'd seen it in movies a hundred times, but movies weren't real. Maybe the holes were from where they injected me with drugs.

Or maybe the holes weren't even there. Maybe I was hallucinating. *Was any of this real?*

Pain suddenly struck me, like a knife twisting in my stomach. I cried out and doubled over in agony. I stumbled back to the fridge and yanked the door open, but there wasn't any more meat. *Why was I looking for meat?*

Pain struck again and I fell to my knees, gasping for air. It felt like I was dying. *Was I? Had I been poisoned?* I squeezed my eyes shut and tried to think. *I should go to the hospital. I should call 911. And say what? That I just woke up and found my bed covered in blood and my face magically healed?*

"Fuck!" I shouted, slamming my hand against the floor. Pain struck again, even stronger than before. My back arched and I retched, but all that came up was a splatter of blood. Over and over, it hit me, twisting my insides until I felt as though I would pass out. Then it was over.

I opened my eyes and saw the ground beef wrapper on the floor, and I acted without thinking. I pushed to my feet and quickly grabbed my sweatshirt off the hook by the door. I zipped it up to cover my torn, bloodstained shirt, then grabbed my backpack from where it still lay open on the floor and shoved my phone into it before rushing out the door.

CHAPTER 5

The third floor lights were still out, and it wasn't until I stepped back into the light on the second floor that I realized I'd been able to see clearly in the darkness. I hurried down the remaining stairs, and when I stepped outside into the night air, I stumbled to a halt.

I could see everything. *Smell* everything. My street was empty at this hour, but I could hear traffic from a couple streets over. I could hear bits of conversation, even though there was no one in sight. The air felt strange against my skin, and I could feel all the hair on my arms stand up. I could actually *feel* it.

I started walking, my eyes darting all over the place on the lookout for my attacker. I hurried for three blocks, then cut through the park, and it was only when the lit up parking lot came into sight that I realized I'd walked to the grocery store.

I pulled my hood up before walking inside, aware that it made me look suspicious, but feeling the need to hide myself. I went straight to the meat department at the back of the store, and when I saw the cold cases of raw meat, the pain in my stomach returned. *Oh God! Not now!*

I started grabbing packages from the case at random. When I had as much as I could carry, I stumbled to the front of the store. I could smell the clerk before I could see him. He smelled like sweat and cigarettes. *And blood.*

I could hear his blood rushing through his veins, and it called to me. I felt a sharp pain in my gums and the metallic taste of blood filled my mouth. I clenched my jaw, keeping my lips firmly closed.

I rounded the corner of the aisle and saw him standing behind the counter. I could see his pulse beating at the base of his neck, and unwillingly my lips parted. So I ran. Clutching the meat to my chest, I ran straight past him and out the door.

"Hey!" he yelled. But I was gone.

Before I knew it, I was back in the park. I dropped my stolen goods, all but one package. I tore into it, not even knowing what it was, and devoured it, then a second package. Afterwards, I leaned against a tree to catch my breath. Nausea hit me, and I bent over and threw everything up. When I was done puking, I straightened and wiped my face with my sleeve. Then I heard a woman scream.

The sound was quickly silenced, but I could hear movement. Without thinking, I ran towards the sound. It all happened in a matter of seconds. I saw him on top of her, holding her down, and my vision went red. I was upon them in an instant, and in one fluid movement I yanked him off her and sank my teeth into his neck. We fell to the ground together, my body landing on top of his. He didn't even struggle as I tore at his flesh. I was in a frenzy, until I wasn't. A feeling of warmth swept over me, calming me. I shuddered and lifted my head, pulling my teeth from his neck. I sat up, straddling his body and slowly licked my lips. The satisfaction I felt at that moment was indescribable. I closed my eyes for a moment, savoring the feeling, until I heard a noise behind me.

My eyes flew open as I twisted my head to look over my shoulder. The woman laying on the ground behind me was pushing herself up into a sitting position. Our eyes met, and hers widened, and then she began to scream.

I meant to tell her she was safe, but my vision narrowed to the smear of blood on her lower lip and I lost myself to the madness once more.

I flew at her, and when my teeth were mere inches from her neck, I slammed into a solid wall and was flung backwards through the air. I hit the ground hard and slid several feet before stopping. I blinked up at the sky, momentarily stunned, then I pushed myself up into a sitting position and looked around.

A figure was hunched over the woman, who had fallen silent. Before I had a chance to react, he stood up and spun around to face me.

"What were you thinking?" he hissed.

My eyes went to his mouth, which was smeared with blood. I looked past him to the woman on the ground.

"You killed her," I whispered shakily.

"Of course I didn't kill her." He scowled and wiped his mouth with the back of his hand. "But you killed him." He waved a hand towards the body on the ground between us.

"I-" I only managed one word before my body started to shake uncontrollably.

He took a quick step towards me and I scrambled backwards, holding up a hand to ward him off. He froze.

The woman on the ground moaned, and I jerked my head to look at her.

"Where is your sire?" the man snapped, causing me to jerk my head back towards him.

"She's alive!" I exclaimed, pointing at the woman.

"As I said." His tone was impatient. He took another step towards me. "*Where* is your sire?"

"I- What?" My eyes darted back and forth between him and the woman.

A police siren pierced the air, causing me to jump. I lept to my feet, and in one quick motion he grabbed me and yanked me hard against his body, his arms going around me. We shot up into the air so fast I didn't have a chance to scream.

I squeezed my eyes shut and clung to him, as the wind tore past us, yanking at my clothes and my hair. Then we were falling. It was like being on a roller coaster. My stomach was in my throat, and I clenched my jaw hard, trying not to vomit. A second later we hit the ground with a jarring thud.

He let go of me and I tumbled off of him and landed on the ground. I was gasping, struggling to breathe. I lay flat on the ground, my hands clenching the tall grass, trying to anchor myself to the earth.

"You are unaccustomed to flying." He said it as a statement, not a question. Still clinging to the grass, I opened my eyes and looked up at him. He bent and reached towards me.

"No!" The word burst out of me, causing him to freeze.

He straightened and let his hand fall to his side. "What you're feeling will pass."

He was right. I was beginning to feel better already. I let go of the grass and slowly sat up. I glanced up at him, towering over me, and quickly climbed to my feet. I brushed my hair out of my face and really looked at him, the sight nearly stopping my heart.

He was beautiful. There was no other word to describe him. He was several inches taller than me, with pale skin and messy brown curls. His blue-gray eyes held my gaze with a hypnotic intensity. I knew I should be afraid, but for some reason I wasn't.

"You're a vampire," I whispered, no longer able to deny the truth.

"As are you." His voice was calm, but his eyes were sharp.

I'm a vampire. The thought made my head spin, and I struggled to remain calm. "Why did you bring me here?"

"My name is Adam."

I stared at him waiting for more, but that was it. "Why did you bring me here?" I asked again.

"Should I have left you in the park with the man you just killed? The way that woman was screaming, you would have been discovered in no time. Unless you killed her as well. Killing a human is punishable by death, as you know." He looked at me, as if expecting a response, and I stared back at him with wide eyes.

His eyes narrowed. "*Did* you know?" When I just continued to stare at him, he frowned. "Where is your sire?"

"I- I don't know what you mean," I stammered.

He took a step closer, causing me to take a step back.

"I'm sorry." He held up a hand. "I don't mean to frighten you, but finding a newborn alone is concerning for several reasons."

"Newborn?" I asked, my voice cracking. Then the words started pouring out of me. "I don't know what you're talking about. I don't know what's happening to me. This isn't real! None of this is real!"

"It's alright," he said gently. "Why don't we go inside and you can tell me all about it."

"Inside?" I repeated dumbly.

He looked past me, and I turned around to see a two-story house, its white paint peeling with age and neglect. The front porch was half hidden by vines, and the windows were boarded up. I'd thought we landed in a meadow, but it was really the overgrown lawn in front of this dilapidated house.

"In there?" I asked, my voice barely a squeak. It was a house out of a horror movie. Someplace only a serial killer would live. Or a vampire.

He chuckled. "It's not so bad on the inside. Come on." He walked past me, not bothering to see if I followed.

I watched him walk towards the house, then I looked around at the dark forest surrounding me. *Where was I?* Deciding I didn't have too many options, I started after him.

CHAPTER 6

I followed him up the rickety steps, into the house. The entryway was small, with a narrow staircase on the right and a long hallway leading toward the back of the house. Directly to the left was a doorway, which he passed through. I followed him into the room, stopping just inside the door to look around.

The age of the house was evident in the warped floorboards and peeling wallpaper, but it was clean and somewhat furnished. A long sofa with a sheet draped over it took up most of the room. There was a fireplace on the far wall, and in front of it was a small wooden table with two chairs. Long dark drapes covered the windows, but unlike the rest of the room, they looked new.

He waved a hand towards the couch. "Please, sit down."

I walked over and sat, watching him warily. The whole situation seemed surreal. He picked up a wooden chair from in front of the fireplace and carried it over, placing it across from me.

He sat down and looked at me expectantly. "Tell me everything."

So I did. I told him about the attack in my apartment, and how I woke up the next day alone and horribly sick. I told him about how the wounds on my face had magically healed, then I had to backtrack and tell him about being attacked on the street a few days before. I told him about my trip to the grocery store, and what happened in the park.

"I killed a man." My hands began to shake as I remembered.

"It's okay," he said soothingly.

I leaned back against the couch. "This is crazy."

He studied me for a moment. "What's your name?"

I blinked. "Sarah."

"Well, Sarah, there are so many things wrong with what you just told me, I'm not sure where to begin." He leaned back in his chair and ran a hand through his hair. "There are laws in the vampire world that protect us and keep us hidden from humans. To change a human without their consent is forbidden. To change a human without the consent of the Strategoi is forbidden."

"The Strategoi?" I repeated, trying to wrap my head around what he was telling me.

"The Strategoi. The high council, made up of the eight most powerful vampires. They are our Supreme Court, if you will, and almost every trial ends with execution." He rolled his eyes. "Another law, and this one *definitely* pertains to you, is that a vampire cannot abandon a newborn.

"A newborn?"

"When a human is turned into a vampire, they are called newborn. The vampire that changed them becomes their sire.

It's your sire's responsibility to teach you..." he paused and shrugged. "Well, how to be a vampire. These mentor relationships last for decades, if not centuries."

"Where's your sire?" I asked, hoping another vampire wasn't about to appear.

He smiled slightly. "I'm well past that point. My sire and I parted ways eons ago."

Well. "How old are you?"

"Old." He sighed and straightened in his chair. "I don't think you're grasping the real problem here."

"Other than the fact that I'm a vampire?" The words came out more sarcastically than I intended.

He gave me a look. "To change a human without permission from the Strategoi is punishable by death. When that happens, they will either kill the newborn, or appoint them a new sire."

I clenched my hands into fists to keep them from shaking. "How would they find out?"

"Just look at you." He waved a hand in my direction. "You killed a human in public. The Strategoi have eyes everywhere. They *will* find you, there's no doubt about that."

"But this isn't my fault!" I cried, jumping up from the couch. "I didn't ask for this!"

"Calm down," he said, standing. "You can stay here tonight while you figure things out."

"With you?" I looked at him incredulously.

His eyebrows shot up. "Do you have a better idea?"

I hesitated, but he was right. I had no other options.

"Okay." I finally said. "Thanks."

"Come on, I'll show you your room."

"My room?"

"Well, technically it's my room-" My eyes shot to his, and he laughed. "No, not like that. There's only one furnished bedroom. I'm not used to having houseguests."

"I can't take your room."

"Of course you can. I'll take the couch."

"But-"

"I'll take the couch," he said firmly. "It would be better if I stay down here, closer to the door, in case anyone else arrives. The Strategoi might already know of your existence."

That was all I needed to hear. Put me in the bedroom. Put me as far from the front door as possible. I nodded my agreement. "Okay. Thanks."

As if in a trance, I followed him upstairs and down the hall to the bedroom. He opened the door and motioned for me to enter, and I stepped into the room and looked around. A large four poster bed took up most of the space, covered in a dark blue comforter that matched the floor to ceiling curtains covering the far wall. The bedding and curtains looked new, but the furniture looked like antiques. Against the wall next to the door was a small dresser with an old, oval mirror hanging above it.

"The bathroom is through there, if you want to get washed up." He pointed to a door to the left. "There's no hot water, but the cold won't bother you now. You can borrow something of mine if you want to change your clothes." He waved a hand towards the dresser. "They obviously won't fit well, but they'll be clean."

"Thanks," I murmured. We stood there a moment, looking at each other. Then he nodded and walked out of the room, closing the door behind him.

I don't know how long I stood there. It could have been a minute, it could have been an hour. Eventually a noise roused me from my stupor, a soft ticking sound. I turned my head towards it and saw an old-fashioned pocket watch laying on the dresser. I walked over to look at it, and when I caught sight of myself in the mirror, my eyes widened.

My hair was a snarly mess, with bits of grass stuck in it. My mouth, chin and neck were covered with dried blood, and my shirt was stained with it.

I turned and ran to the bathroom. I saw the clawfoot tub and quickly turned on the water, then I tore off my clothes and jumped in. I sat on my knees and leaned forward, splashing myself with water. It ran off me in dark rivulets, turning the bottom of the tub reddish brown. A sob escaped me and I leaned over and stuck my head under the water.

I scrubbed my hair, then my body, not bothering to look for soap. I scrubbed until the water ran clear, then I tucked my knees up under my chin and wrapped my arms around my legs.

I sat like that for a while, letting the water continue to run. I became lost in thought, reliving all that had happened to me in the last two days. When I thought about Allie, I started to cry.

Tears ran down my cheeks, and I felt one splash on my knee. I looked down at it and saw that it was red. Confused, I rubbed it away with my fingertip and stretched my legs out in front of me. Another red drop fell, landing on my thigh. I wiped at the tears on my cheeks and looked at my hands. *I was crying blood!* The realization only made me cry harder, and soon I was scrubbing myself down again.

I eventually cried myself out, washed myself one last time, and turned off the water. I stood up and grabbed a folded towel off the nearby shelf, wrapping it around me as I stared down at my dirty clothes on the floor. *There was no way I was putting that bloody shirt back on.*

I wandered back into the bedroom and crossed over to the dresser. I looked in the mirror to check for any missed spots of blood, and when I saw myself I froze. My skin was perfectly clean, perfectly smooth too, but it was my eyes that held my attention. They had changed color, and were entirely green now. *Bright* green, like cat eyes. I leaned over the dresser, putting my face close to the mirror, and stared at them with disbelief.

Eventually, I leaned back and let my gaze move over my reflection, searching for any other changes. I looked the same, but also different somehow. My skin looked flawless, except for the two small holes on my neck from where I'd been bitten.

I raised a hand to touch them, wondering why they hadn't healed like the scrapes on my face, then noticed how perfect my hand looked. My hands were normally dry and cracked from constant washing at the diner, and my fingertips calloused from playing my violin. Now they were as smooth and soft as baby skin.

I squeezed them into fists and opened them again, almost expecting them to change back to normal. But they remained soft and perfect. I let out a shaky breath. This would take some getting used to.

I reached down and opened the top dresser drawer. Looking through Adam's things felt like an invasion of his privacy, but I needed clean clothes. The drawer contained neatly folded shirts, and I grabbed one and quickly pulled it over my head, knowing if I thought about it too long I'd chicken out and end up back in my own blood-stained clothes. It was a plain black t-shirt, which hit me mid-thigh.

I found pants in the next drawer, but knew they'd be too big. Luckily there was a pair of gym shorts. I pulled them on and cinched the drawstring at the waist, tying it in a knot to hold them in place.

I stepped back, trying to see my entire body in the mirror. I looked ridiculous. I grabbed the waistband of the shorts and was about to slide them off when I heard a knock at the door.

"Sarah?"

"Yeah?" I called. "Come in." My heart started pounding as the door opened.

Adam stepped into the room, and his eyes moved over me. The corner of his mouth ticked up in a half-smile.

"I'm glad you found something that fits," he said, his hand still on the doorknob.

"Um, yeah." I nervously smoothed the front of my shirt with my hands. "Thanks."

"It's still early. I'd like to talk some more if you're feeling up to it. There are things we need to discuss."

I nodded. "Okay."

I followed him down to the living room and sat on the couch. He took the chair across from me, and stared at me for a few moments before he finally spoke.

"I discovered this property a few months ago," he said, looking around the room. "The drive leading in was mostly swallowed by the forest, telling me no one has been here for years." His eyes met mine. "You're safe here."

"Where did you live before this?" I asked.

"Oh, here and there." He leaned back in his chair. "Vampires move around a lot. If we stay in one place too long, humans start to notice we don't age."

"Oh," I said, not knowing how else to respond.

"You know you can't ever go home, Sarah."

"What?" The word came out louder than I intended.

"You can't go home again." He looked directly into my eyes as he spoke. "If you return to your family, you'll eventually lose control and kill them. Or the Strategoi will find you with them and kill you all. Either way, if you return to them they're as good as dead."

"I'll never see Allie again," I whispered.

"I'm sorry," he said softly. "That's the hardest part about becoming a vampire."

I blinked quickly, trying hard not to cry. The thought of shedding more blood tears was too much to handle.

"Who's Allie?" he asked after a minute.

"My sister." I clenched my hands into fists, digging my fingernails into my palms. "She's the only family I have. My parents are dead."

"I'm sorry." He sounded sincere when he said it. "There's no one else? No husband or boyfriend?"

I laughed harshly. "No." I glanced at him. "What about you? Do you- I mean, do vampires have families?"

"Most do, yes. When a vampire changes a human, they become that person's sire, and the newborn vampire becomes their progeny. A vampire's sire is like a parent, in a weird sort of way, even though they are often your lover as well."

"Gross."

He chuckled. "Yeah, that didn't come out right. It's hard to explain, but if the same vampire changed both you and I, we'd be part of the same family."

"Where's your family?"

"As I told you, my sire and I have parted ways."

"Do you have any vampire siblings? Or progeny? I mean, have you ever changed anyone?"

"I have no family."

His tone told me not to pry, so I changed the subject. "Will sunlight kill me?"

"You? Yes." I looked at him questioningly. "Vampires grow stronger as they age, and can develop a tolerance for sunlight. It takes centuries, mind you. A newborn such as yourself would be killed, but an elder can walk in the sunlight just like a human."

"What else can kill me?"

"Several things, I'm afraid. Fire, beheading, being stabbed through the heart." I shuddered at the thought. "But if you manage to avoid all that, you are indeed immortal."

"Immortal," I murmured.

"You don't sound too impressed."

"Living forever while everyone I know dies? It sounds sad to me. And lonely."

"You have no idea," he said softly.

"And we can fly." I shook my head in amazement.

He smiled slightly. "Like a tolerance for sunlight, it is a skill that's acquired with age.

"Oh." That was disappointing. "What about hypnosis? Can vampires really put people into a trance?"

"That is true, to some extent. When we feed, our fangs produce a venom that will put a human into a drug-like trance. A short while later, the venom wears off and the human should have no memory of what happened."

"What happens when they see the holes in their neck?" I asked, lifting a hand to touch my neck.

"Simply rub a drop of your blood over the wound and it will heal before they wake from their trance."

"My blood?"

He stood and moved to sit on the couch beside me, and I turned my body so I was facing him. His fangs dropped down so quickly, I jerked back against the arm of the couch.

"It's alright," he said softly. He pressed his thumb to the tip of one fang and then held it out for me to see the drop off blood gleaming on it. He reached towards me and I sucked in a breath, holding it.

Our eyes met, and without breaking my gaze, he lifted his hand to my neck and rubbed his thumb over the bite mark. My skin warmed and tingled at his touch. For a moment we stayed like gazing into each other's eyes, his hand cupping my neck. Then he let his hand fall and the spell was broken. I blinked and cleared my throat.

"One drop is all it takes." He looked down at his thumb, which had already healed. "Vampire blood has amazing healing abilities."

"I've noticed." I rubbed a hand over my face, remembering how my wounds had disappeared.

"Now let's talk about you," he said, leaning back against the arm of the couch.

"O-*kay*," I said slowly. There wasn't much to tell. Nothing about my depressing life would fascinate a centuries-old vampire.

"I've given it some thought, and I think you should stay with me a while. I can help you. I can teach you how to live as a vampire, and how to remain undetected by the Strategoi."

"Why would you do that?" I asked. "Wouldn't that put you at risk?"

"It would."

"Then why? You don't even know me, why would you risk your life to help me?"

"Because like you, I was not given a choice. My *sire,*" he said the word with distaste, "did not seek my permission before changing me."

My eyes widened. I don't know what answer I'd been expecting, but it wasn't that.

"And because you were right earlier. Being immortal is lonely." He sounded sad when he said it, but then he laughed. "And *boring*." He rolled his eyes dramatically. "I've been bored for a *century,* Sarah, so stay and let me help you."

I slowly nodded. "Okay. I'll stay."

We spent the next couple of hours in the living room, while I peppered him with questions. "How often do I need to drink blood?" I asked.

"As a newborn you must feed every night." He told me. "But as you age, you will learn to control your hunger and be able to go a night or two without it."

"And I don't have to kill them, right? I can hypnotize them, or whatever, and they'll be fine?"

"Correct. Or you could survive off the blood of animals. It doesn't taste as good, but it does the job."

I swallowed, finding it hard to believe that I'd ever enjoy the taste of blood. Then I remembered how I'd tore into the man in the park and I cringed.

"You'll get used to it," Adam said, as if reading my mind.

"Are there a lot of vampires?" I asked, changing the subject.

He shrugged. "A few million probably."

"A few million!" I exclaimed, dumbfounded. "How do millions of vampires stay hidden from the rest of us?"

"When you remember that there are billions of people in the world, the vampire population is a fraction of a percent."

"Oh." He was right, of course.

"Besides, we don't really *need* to stay hidden. We can walk freely among humans after dark. You've probably encountered a vampire or two without realizing it. Most city dwellers have."

"Vampires don't live in the country?"

"Small towns make for nosy neighbors."

"You're right about that." I muttered.

We continued to talk until he eventually stood and told me it was time to sleep. I looked to the wall of curtains, but not a hint of light peeked through.

"Is the sun coming up?" I asked worriedly.

"Not yet, but soon."

"How- How will I know when it's dark again?" I squeezed my hands together nervously. "What if I wake up and it's still light out?"

He stepped forward and took my hands in his. "I will come for you when it is time. If you need me before then, just call out and I'll hear you." I stared at my hands in his. He was rubbing his thumbs over the backs of my hands, and I was surprised by how good it felt. Then he released me and stepped away. "You are safe with me, Sarah. I promise."

I went upstairs and sat on the edge of the bed. It felt strange climbing into the bed of a stranger, but I didn't feel like sleeping on the floor. Slowly, I lay down, resting my head on his pillow. Immediately, his scent filled my senses, and without thinking I rolled onto my stomach and buried my face in his pillow. I inhaled deeply and desire hit me hard, causing me to grind my hips against the mattress. A growl escaped me and I froze. *Did that sound come out of me?*

I quickly pulled my face out of the pillow and rolled onto my back. I stared up at the ceiling, astonished that I could be aroused after everything I'd just been through, and just from smelling his pillow. *This had to be a vampire thing.* I yanked the pillow out from under my head and tossed it to the bottom of the bed. Then I curled onto my side and prayed for sleep.

CHAPTER 7

Nightmares plagued me, making me relive my attack. Then the dream changed, and I was attacking Allie. I ripped her apart and drank all her blood, then I left her body on the floor in my apartment. Then the dream changed again, and I was standing over my mothers grave. It was night, and it was raining heavily. The rain washed the dirt away, until I could see her coffin, then the coffin opened and my mother crawled out. Her body was half decomposed, and I was terrified. I wanted to run, but my feet were frozen to the ground. She grabbed me with skeletal hands and yanked me to her, then she sank her teeth into my neck.

I woke with a cry, shooting straight up in bed. My heart pounded uncontrollably while my eyes darted around the room, searching for my mother.

"Sarah?" I jerked my head towards the door at the sound of my name. "Are you alright?" It was Adam.

I shook my head quickly, trying to rid my mind of the terrifying image of my mother.

"I'm coming in," he called, as he opened the door. He stepped into the room, his eyes immediately falling on me in bed. "I'm sorry," he said, his hand still on the doorknob. "I heard you cry out..."

I swallowed. "I had a nightmare."

He nodded slowly. "That happens a lot in the beginning. At least, it did to me." He looked away, his expression troubled, as if he were remembering.

"Is it night?" I asked, not wanting to have to go back to sleep. If the nightmares would continue, I didn't ever want to sleep again.

"Yes," he said, looking at me again. Our eyes met and held for a moment, then he cleared his throat and looked away. "I'll be downstairs."

He stepped out of the room and closed the door, and I listened to the sound of his footsteps as he walked away before I threw off the blanket and jumped out of bed. I went into the bathroom to wash my face and brush my hair, before going downstairs. I saw my torn, blood stained clothes on the bathroom floor, and decided to stick with Adam's t-shirt and gym shorts.

When I started down the stairs, I saw Adam in the entryway below. He stood in the open doorway, looking out, and when he heard me approach he turned to look at me. I smiled nervously and continued down the stairs.

"We have a lot to discuss," he said, when I reached the bottom. "But first you need to feed."

My stomach plummeted, and I started shaking my head. "I can't. I'm not ready. What if I end up killing them? I can't kill another person." But even as I said the words, my lips trembled with anticipation.

Adam held up his hands to stop me. "Calm down. There isn't anyone within miles of this place. Vampires can survive perfectly well on animal blood, and the surrounding forest is full of them. Come on." He turned and walked out the door, and I took a deep breath to steady myself before following him outside.

When I stepped out into the night air, my senses came alive. The stars sparkled like diamonds, and the breeze against my skin was a caress that made the hair on the back of my neck stand up with pleasure.

"Are you ready?" Adam asked, startling me.

"What?" I jerked my head to look at him. "No!"

He smiled reassuringly. "You'll be fine."

I shook my head. "I'm not ready."

He walked over to me and took both of my hands in his. I looked down at our joined hands, then back at him.

"You need to feed, Sarah. If you go too long without it, your vampire instincts will take over and you'll lose control. That's when bad things happen."

"But I threw up all the meat I ate," I reminded him.

"Vampires need fresh blood to survive, not old processed meat. That's why you threw up."

Oh.

"Now close your eyes," he said.

I narrowed my eyes at him.

"Close your eyes," he repeated, giving my hands a squeeze. I did as instructed, and he released my hands. "Now listen."

At first all I could hear was my heartbeat, pounding in my ears. It sounded too loud, and too fast.

"Be calm," he murmured. "Focus on my heartbeat."

"I don't think I can do this," I said, but then I heard it. It was slow, and steady. I could feel my body relax as my heartbeat slowed to match his. After a minute our hearts and our breathing were completely in sync.

"Now what do you hear?" he asked softly.

"The wind," I said, keeping my eyes closed. The wind sounded like music, far off in the distance. But there was *so* much more. "I hear frogs. And there are mice in the grass. There's something in the woods." I turned my face towards the sound, and hunger hit me.

Without thinking, I opened my eyes and ran towards the woods. I darted into the trees, dodging branches as I cut through the underbrush in search of my prey. I moved with a speed that shouldn't have been possible, and leapt onto the animal before it even knew I was there.

Kneeling on the ground, I gripped its body tightly as I sank my fangs into it. I sucked deeply, letting my eyes close as warm satisfaction poured over me. I drained it quickly, then pulled my fangs free and licked the blood from my lips. My tongue scraped over my fangs, and I shuddered with pleasure. Then I opened my eyes and saw what I had done.

Regret consumed me as I looked down at the rabbit in my hands. I'd been so lost in my hunger, I hadn't fully realized what I was doing, but looking at its small, lifeless body made me want to cry. I sank back on my heels, and ran my hand over its soft, brown fur, and I felt heartbroken.

I heard Adam approach, and I looked up at him through the red shimmer of tears. He crouched beside me, and lifted the rabbit out of my hands and gently lay it on the ground.

"It's okay," he said softly, taking me by the hands. He stood, pulling me up with him. "We feed to survive. It's no different from a human eating a steak."

I looked up at him. "I don't know why I'm so upset. I didn't even cry when I killed that man. But this feels different."

"That man had it coming, Sarah. He didn't deserve your tears."

I looked at the rabbit. "It was so helpless. Rabbits are so gentle, and I-" I broke off on a sob, and Adam pulled me into his embrace. I rested my head on his chest, as if it were the most natural thing in the world, and let him hold me while I cried myself out.

He rubbed my back, not caring that I soaked his shirt with bloody tears. When I finally stopped crying, I pulled back and looked up at him.

"Thank you," I murmured, sniffing.

"You don't have to thank me," he said softly. "Come, let's go back to the house."

"We can't just leave her," I said, looking down at the rabbit. And suddenly I realized why I was so upset. The rabbit was Allie. Soft and gentle, innocent, and completely undeserving its terrible fate.

Without a word, Adam sank to the ground. He thrust his hands into the earth, pushing through the vegetation and dirt as if it were nothing. I watched, stunned, as he dug a hole with his bare hands, and buried the rabbit. When he was done, he stood and brushed his hands on his pants.

"Thank you," I said. "I know it's foolish-"

"It's not," he said, interrupting me. "Nothing about you is foolish."

I looked away, embarrassed, but also pleased by his words. I turned and started back towards the house, hyper-aware of his presence as he followed. I was puzzled by how comfortable I felt with him. He was a stranger, and a vampire. I should have been terrified, but for some reason I felt safe. *He* felt safe.

By the time we stepped out of the woods, I'd calmed considerably. "I think I want to stay outside a while longer," I said, as we neared the house.

"Do you want company?" he asked.

"Sure." He sat down on the porch steps, but I remained standing. "Thank you," I said, without looking at him. "For being so understanding, and for helping me and letting me stay here." I shot him a glance and saw that he was watching me. I looked around, taking in my surroundings. "Everything looks so different. Everything shimmers. It's so beautiful." I looked up at the sky. "Do you ever get used to it?"

He leaned back on his elbows and tipped his head back to look up at the sky. "Eventually. It took years for the newness to wear off. Now, I'd give anything to see a sunrise."

I looked at him. "But some vampires can go out in the sun, right?"

"Yes, but it will be a long time before I reach that point."

I walked over and sat on the steps next to him, and leaned back on my elbows to look up at the sky. We stayed that way for over an hour, with neither of us speaking. It should have been awkward, sitting in silence with a stranger like that, but it wasn't.

Eventually my thoughts turned back to the problem at hand, *me being a vampire*, and I spoke, breaking the comfortable silence between us.

"I've replayed everything, over and over again, trying to make sense of it all. I can't stop thinking about the vampire that attacked me." I turned my head to look at him. "Why bother changing me just to abandon me? If they just wanted to feed, why didn't they put me in a trance or whatever, and heal the wounds from their bite? Or kill me, right?"

He frowned. "The thing is, changing a human involves more than just feeding from them. It's not something that can happen by accident."

I thought for a moment. "Maybe they planned on coming back later, except I went to the store and then ended up here with you? They could be at my apartment right now, waiting for me."

He shook his head. "That doesn't seem likely. As your sire, they are completely responsible for you. Which means they would be held responsible for any trouble you caused."

"Trouble, like what happened in the park," I said, my mind racing.

"Exactly. Every vampire remembers what it is like to be a newborn. That initial hunger..." His voice trailed off as if he were remembering. "Leaving a newborn to fend for themselves is to release a terror upon the world. Which would *definitely* draw notice from the human authorities. Which is exactly why abandoning a newborn is forbidden."

"Who would do that?" I asked. "Who would risk angering the, um, Strategoi like that?"

"Someone who had nothing to lose."

"What do you mean?"

"There are criminals in the vampire world, just like in the human world," he explained. "Rogue vampires who like to stir up trouble. Not everyone is content living under the Strategoi's command."

"So a criminal vampire changed me without consent to piss off the Strategoi?"

He shrugged. "It's possible."

I slowly shook my head. "I might never know who did this."

"I hope you never find out, Sarah, because that means that whoever did this to you never finds you."

He was right, but going the rest of my existence without answers was going to make me crazy. I sighed and looked back up at the sky. We fell back into silence for a while, but I was no longer able to enjoy it.

"I think I'm going to bed," I finally said, standing. "I mean, I just need to be alone for a while." I hesitated. "Um-" I broke off, not knowing what to say.

"Call out if you need anything," he said, understanding. "I'll be nearby."

"Thanks." I exhaled with relief and went inside. I spent the rest of the night laying in bed, staring at the ceiling, trying to come up with an explanation for why a vampire would change me. I eventually drifted off, and thankfully, did not dream.

CHAPTER 8

When I woke, the house was silent. I climbed out of bed and crossed to the dresser to look at Adam's pocket watch. The time said 7:30, but if that was am or pm, I had no way of knowing. I went into the bathroom and washed my face, and used Adam's hairbrush to tame my hair, then I went back to the dresser to check the time again. 7:36. A moment later there was a knock at the door.

"Sarah?" Adam's voice came from the hall.

I opened the door and saw him standing in the hallway. "Hey."

He smiled softly. "It's night. I hope you were able to rest?"

I nodded. "Yeah, I just woke up."

"You'll find that you'll naturally wake up each night shortly after the sun sets, and you'll instinctively know when sunrise is coming. You'll get the hang of it."

"Good to know," I said, feeling relieved.

He seemed to hesitate before speaking again. "I know you don't want to hear this, but you need to feed again." I started to shake my head, and he touched my arm. "You *have* to, Sarah. If you don't feed every night, you'll lose control."

I clenched my jaw, knowing he was right. I couldn't risk losing control. I was still shook up over the rabbit, but it was preferable to killing a human.

"I'll be with you the entire time," he said, rubbing my arm once before letting his hand fall. "Come on." He turned and started down the hall, and I reluctantly followed him.

As they did every time, my senses came alive when I stepped outside. I lifted my face and inhaled deeply, loving the feel of the night air on my skin. I looked up at the sky, and became momentarily lost in the stars. It was like being in a Van Gough painting.

"Are you ready?" Adam asked.

I pulled my attention from the stars and gave him a wry look. "Not really."

He chuckled, and took me by the hands, just like the night before. "Close your eyes and listen."

I reluctantly closed my eyes, and my heart immediately began to pound faster.

"Slow down," he murmured. "Calm your heart."

I frowned, and tried to focus. Then a breeze blew by, pushing his scent at me. Without realizing what I was doing, I inhaled deeply, and was surprised to feel desire stir. I tried to push the feeling away, but the harder I tried, the more it grew.

"What do you hear?" Adam asked, oblivious to what I was going through.

"Um," I tried to listen, but all I could hear was his heartbeat. Heat swirled low in my stomach, and I felt myself sway towards him.

"Listen."

I strained my ears, and then I heard it. Hunger hit me, and my eyes shot open. Adam's eyes were completely black, and his lips were parted, revealing his fangs. I felt my body tighten.

His lips curled. "Go."

I ran into the woods, jumping over roots and dodging trees, vaguely aware that Adam had joined me. I saw the deer only a second before I leapt, tackling one to the ground. I had my teeth in its neck before the other two even noticed my arrival. It kicked and thrashed, but it was no match for me. I closed my eyes, feeling its life pour into me. For a few moments we were one. Its heartbeat was my own. Then it was over.

I released the dead animal and sat up. Adam sat a few feet away, leaning against the trunk of a tree, a dead deer in front of him. He had blood on his lips, and the sight made my body clench. He grinned, and to my surprise, I grinned back.

Tonight was different. I didn't feel sad like before, I felt alive and full of energy. I wanted to run, and jump. To fly even.

Adam stood and offered me a hand. "You did well."

I took his hand and he pulled me to my feet. "Thanks," I said, breathlessly. My body was thrumming with energy, and I had to let it out somehow. "I want to run," I blurted.

He blinked with surprise, then his lips slowly curved. "Then let's run."

I laughed, and took off. I moved so quickly, the trees passed by in a blur. The only thing that remained in focus was Adam, running beside me.

We ran for hours, cutting through the forest, and across open fields. We crossed a river in one leap, and I shrieked with joy, feeling more alive than I could ever remember.

We eventually returned to the house, and spent the last few hours of the night talking on the front steps. I asked Adam about his life before becoming a vampire, and he regaled me with stories of his childhood, of all the pranks he played on his poor butler, and how he teased his sister mercilessly.

I laughed, amused by his stories. Then he told me about his father's death, and the mood sobered.

"I became the new lord," he said, staring off into the distance. "I inherited the entire estate, and the massive fortune that came with it. That's why my sire chose me. Vampires collect wealthy humans, and claim their wealth and holdings to make themselves more powerful." He looked at me, and I was taken aback by the anger in his eyes. But there was pain there, as well.

I covered his hand with mine, and he looked down at it. Then he turned his hand over and laced his fingers through mine. I watched the emotions play across his face, then I surprised us both by sliding closer to him and resting my head on his shoulder.

I don't know what made me do it. I'd only wanted to comfort him. But as I listened to his heartbeat calm, I realized there was more to it than that. I felt an overwhelming urge to be close to him. To touch him. My feelings made no sense, but *nothing* about being a vampire made sense.

CHAPTER 9

A noise woke me. I opened my eyes and saw him standing in the doorway. He started towards me, yanking his shirt off as he approached, and I sat up, savoring the sight of him. When he reached the bed I grabbed him and pulled him to me. He crushed his mouth against mine, parting my lips with his tongue, and I moaned, arching against him.

He pulled away, only to grab the hem of my shirt and pull it over my head. His eyes moved over me, and my nipples hardened in response. He lowered his head to take one in his mouth, running his tongue over it before sucking, and I fisted my hands in his hair and held him tight against me. He released my nipple and claimed my mouth once more, pushing me back against the mattress and grinding his hips against me. God, yes. I was ready.

I reached down and unfastened his pants, pushing them down as far as I could without breaking our kiss, but he pulled back, breaking it anyway. I lifted my head and tried to kiss him again but he placed a hand on my neck and gently pushed me back down. He nudged my chin with his thumb, guiding my head to the side. Then he lowered his head and ran his tongue up the side of my neck.

"Please," I begged, lifting one leg to wrap around him.

He gently lowered my leg from around his waist and slid my shorts off. I lifted my hips to make it easier for him, and his lips parted, revealing his fangs. He slid his pants the rest of the way off and lowered himself onto me, settling his body between my legs. I moaned at the feel of his hardness pressed against me and spread my legs wider for him. I was already wet, and desperate to have him inside of me. Slowly he arched his hips, sliding his cock against me, making my body throb with pleasure.

"Please!" I gasped, digging my nails into him. He kissed me again, nibbling on my lips before sliding his tongue into my mouth. Then he grabbed my ass with one hand, lifting my hips off the bed as he slid into me.

I whimpered and rocked against him, my body tightening as he slid into me over and over. He moved slowly, teasing me, and I grabbed his hips and ground hard against him.

"Please Adam!" I gasped, wanting more. He growled when I said his name and thrust harder, faster.

My fangs came down when I climaxed. I cried out as my body tightened around him, then again as he sank his fangs into my neck.

The sound of my cry woke me. My heart was pounding in my chest and my fists were twisted in the sheets. My body was still throbbing from my orgasm, and I lay there a moment in shock. I'd never had an orgasm in my sleep before. Then a thought struck me. *Did Adam hear me cry out?*

I sat up, overcome with embarrassment. I strained my ears listening for any sound, but there was nothing. I wondered if it was dark out yet, but a quick glance at the curtains revealed nothing. I slid off the bed and crossed the room to open the door and peek out into the hallway.

"Adam?" The second I said his name he appeared at the end of the hall, startling me. "Is it night?" I asked.

He nodded once. "Did you sleep well?"

"Yeah." I was so embarrassed about my dream, I could barely look at him. *Was I blushing? Could vampires blush?*

"Come down," he said, already turning to head back downstairs.

I waited until he was out of sight, then frantically combed through my hair with my fingers before following him down.

We went right out onto the lawn, where he once again urged me to be calm and listen. It was difficult to concentrate, with my body still feeling the effects of my dream, but eventually I was able to focus. I heard the wind, the frogs, and the mice. And something more. I barely gave Adam a glance before I tore off into the woods.

The trees were a blur as I ran by, but I hardly noticed. All of my senses were focused on my prey. This was no deer to be caught unaware. It knew I was coming. Flight or fight, what would it be?

The huge owl flew out of the trees just ahead of me and time seemed to slow as I leapt up and snatched it from the sky. Its talons tore into my chest as I sank my fangs into it, its great wings beating against my head as we fell towards the ground. Once, twice, then no more. By the time I hit the ground the bird had gone still.

I pulled my fangs free and looked down at the owl, and a flood of emotion rushed through me. Satisfaction, of course, but also sorrow. Like me, this was a creature of the night. A predator that must kill to survive. I crouched and laid the owl on the ground. I gently ran my hand over its feathers, surprised by how soft they were.

"Impressive," Adam said, appearing at my side.

I stood and wiped my hands on my shorts. "Why did it fight me? I thought my venom was supposed to drug it?"

"Our venom only works on humans, I'm afraid."

"Oh." I looked around then, finally noticing my surroundings.

The forest stood behind us, but to the front was a wide open space with a large pond in the middle. Beyond the pond the ground rose to a tree-covered hillside. It was a secluded spot, and it was beautiful.

"Care for a swim?" Adam asked, raising his eyebrows at me.

I narrowed my eyes at him. "I don't have a swimsuit."

He flashed me a smile that was pure sin. "Neither do I."

I'm about to go skinny dipping with a hot vampire. No big deal. I stared at Adam's back as he led the way to the water. He yanked his shirt off as he neared the edge and my eyes widened.

His shoulders were wide and his back was muscular, but that wasn't what took my breath away. It was the tangle of scars that covered his back from his shoulders to his waist. I gasped, and he looked over his shoulder at me.

His smile died when he saw my expression. "Oh. Yeah." He shrugged and turned to face me. "I guess I should've warned you about that."

"What happened?" I asked, trying not to stare at his bare chest.

"My sire tried to teach me obedience." He rolled his eyes, as if it were merely an annoyance.

I shook my head. "I don't understand. Why didn't you heal?"

"It's not a fun story, and I'd rather swim than tell it."

"But-"

"*Especially* since you don't have a swimsuit." The corner of his mouth curled, and he turned back around and continued towards the water.

My heart began to pound, and I fought to calm it, knowing he could probably hear it. I swallowed and followed him to the water. When he reached the edge, he kicked off his shoes, and with his back still to me, he slid his pants off and tossed them to the side. I stumbled to a halt at the sight of him. He walked into the water until it came up to his waist, then dove under the surface.

"Oh my god," I said aloud. "I can't believe this is happening." I hurried to the edge of the pond and yanked my clothes off as fast as I could. I rushed into the water, bracing for the initial cold, but found myself pleasantly surprised by how comfortable it felt.

"I love this place," Adam said, startling me. He had resurfaced a few feet away.

I yelped and ducked down in the water to hide my nakedness. He grinned and splashed me, and I laughed and splashed him back. He wiped the water from his face, still grinning, then he leaned back into the water and floated away. I watched him drift a moment, before swimming after him.

When I reached his side, he lifted his head to look at me. I stretched my feet down to see if I could touch the bottom, and the water came up to my nose. I kicked off the bottom and started treading water.

My eyes widened as Adam swam over and took me in his arms, holding me up to keep my face out of the water. My naked skin slid against his and I clenched my jaw to keep myself from moaning.

He held me close, our faces inches apart, and I stared into his eyes. His hardness pressed against me, making heat pool in my stomach. I should say no. I should move away. I didn't know anything about him, except that he was deadly. But I was deadly too now, and I wanted him like I've never wanted anyone before.

Before I could change my mind, I wrapped my arms around his neck and pressed my mouth to his. He groaned and ran his tongue across my lips, and I parted them, allowing him inside. I rocked against him, and his hands slid down to cup my ass. He lifted me higher, and I wrapped my legs around his waist, pressing myself against his cock. He devoured me with his mouth, kissing me until I could barely breathe.

I leaned on his shoulders to lift myself up, sliding myself against the length of his cock. *Fuck, that felt good.* I slid again and again, faster each time, my frantic movement making the water splash around us. I could feel the tension building inside of me, and I chased it. I couldn't believe how fast it was happening, I'd never felt anything like it before.

The next time I slid up his body he moved his hips and brought me down onto his cock. I cried out as I sank onto him, and ground forward rubbing my clit against him. I gasped his name as I began to ride him. He kissed my neck and my shoulders, scraping my flesh with his fangs as he thrust into me. My body was on fire, the tension inside of me winding tighter and tighter. I gasped and whimpered with every thrust, amazed by how fast my body was responding.

"That's it," he murmured, lifting his head from my neck to look into my eyes. For a split second, I wondered if my eyes were as black as his. Then my orgasm ripped through me with a force that erased all thought. There was nothing left but instinct.

I lunged forward and sank my fangs into his neck. I sucked hard, drawing his blood into me, and his movements quickened, his cock pounding into me with brutal force. I could feel his heartbeat, his very essence throughout my entire body. Pleasure hit me in waves, over and over, never giving me a moment to catch my breath. I closed my eyes and stars exploded behind my eyelids.

Adam groaned, and I could feel his cock pulsing inside of me as he came. I pulled my fangs free and lifted my head to look at him. His eyes were closed, but he opened them and they went straight to my mouth. He leaned in and licked the blood from my lips, growling softly.

I pressed my forehead to his and closed my eyes. He held me close, with my legs still wrapped around him and his cock still inside me. We stayed that way for the longest time, but eventually the euphoria began to wear off and the reality of what I'd done sank in. *I bit him.*

I lifted my head to look at him. "I'm sorry," I said, looking at the bite mark on his neck.

"Don't be," he said, his voice rough.

"I don't know why I did that."

"It's natural," he said, as he finally slid his cock out of me. "Most vampires feed during sex."

I felt a loss as his cock left my body and immediately wanted more from him. The corner of his mouth lifted, as if he knew exactly what I was thinking.

I unwrapped myself from around him and pushed away. He let me go, and I swam towards shore a little until I could stand with my head and shoulders out of the water.

"Did you want to bite me?" I asked, without looking at him. "Yes."

I looked at him then. "Do you still want to?"

He stared at me a moment before answering. *"Yes."*

He fucked me two more times in the water, making me come harder each time. When he sank his teeth into me the first time I expected pain, but instead I felt pleasure like nothing I'd ever known. The feel of his lips pulling the blood from my body made me come so hard I almost passed out. Stars danced behind my eyelids again and reality ceased to exist. It was just the two of us. My blood flowing into him, and his blood flowing into me. Our hearts were beating as one.

When it was over I could barely walk out of the water. I felt warm, and tingly, and slightly high. His blood was like a drug, and I was addicted. I laughed aloud at the thought, and he looked at me curiously.

"This is crazy," I said, as I got dressed.

"What is?" He'd managed to put his clothes on faster than me.

I looked at him for a moment, not knowing what to say, then I shook my head. "Nothing."

We walked back to the house in silence. It should have felt awkward, considering I'd only known him a couple days, but it wasn't. I felt completely at ease.

It took a while to get back. I didn't realize how far I ran when I was after the owl. When we arrived at the house, we sat on the front steps and spent the rest of the night talking. I told him about my life. My happy childhood, followed by my tragic teen years with my mom's illness and my dad's suicide. When I talked about Allie, I started to cry. He wiped the tears from my face and held me.

"Losing someone who is still alive is often harder than losing someone to death," he told me, stroking my hair as I snuggled against his chest. We sat on the steps for the rest of the night, leaning against each other.

"It's time," he eventually said, pressing a kiss to my hair. I leaned back and looked up into his eyes. So many emotions ran through me at that moment, all I could do was nod.

We walked into the house hand-in-hand, and at the bottom of the stairs he leaned in and kissed my cheek.

"Sleep well," he said, starting to release my hand.

I gripped his hand tighter, and he stilled. "You don't have to sleep on the couch," I said softly.

He looked at me for a moment, his expression unreadable. Then he nodded.

Neither of us spoke as we walked up to the bedroom. My emotions were in a jumble as I climbed into bed. I felt shy, nervous, and excited all at once. I slid beneath the covers and looked at Adam. He stood near the bed, watching me. Then he slowly began to undress.

I watched him, savoring the sight. Once he was down to his black boxer briefs, he slid into bed beside me. He lay on his side, and pulled me closer, until my back was snug against his chest, then he draped his arm over my waist and rested his head on the pillow above mine.

I snuggled closer, loving the feel of his body spooning mine. My nervousness vanished, and I smiled to myself as I closed my eyes.

This was the first time in my life I'd actually *slept* with a man. I'd had a few casual flings, but never felt close enough to someone to let them spend the night. And here I was, sharing a bed with a vampire I'd only known a few days.

There was *something* about him. He was basically a stran but sex with him had felt so natural. And the way we could spend hours together without talking, I'd never been able to do that with anyone. I felt safe with him. I felt content, and at peace.

I listened to his heartbeat slow, until I thought he was asleep. But then he spoke.

"Thank you," he whispered against my hair.

I opened my eyes. "For what?"

"For tonight. For being here with me. For making me feel alive again."

I didn't know what to say, but he didn't seem to be waiting for an answer. A few moments later his breathing deepened and I knew he was asleep.

His words affected me, and I lay in the darkness, staring at the far wall, until the sound of his heartbeat eventually lulled me to sleep.

ger,

CHAPTER 10

I heard Adam say my name, and I mumbled into my pillow, not wanting to let go of my delicious dream.

"Come on," he said, gently slapping my butt through the blankets. "I have a fun night planned."

I released the pillow and rolled onto my back to look up at him, and he chuckled and started for the door.

"I'll be downstairs," he said, on his way out of the room.

I watched him go, then I threw off the blankets and leapt out of bed. I hurried into the bathroom for a quick, cold bath, and when I reached for a towel, I saw my clothes folded neatly on the shelf. Adam had washed them for me. I dried off quickly and put on my jeans and hoodie. Then I ran Adam's brush through my hair and headed down. He was waiting for me at the bottom of the stairs.

"Hey," I said, as I descended the stairs.

He smiled at me. "Hey."

Damn, he was gorgeous. I wanted to throw myself at him, and lick him and bite him. I cleared my throat. "Thanks for washing my clothes."

"Of course." He casually shoved his hands in his pants pockets. "I'm afraid your t-shirt was beyond repair."

I huffed. "I bet."

He raised his eyebrows at me. "Hungry?"

"Always."

"Good. I have a special treat for you tonight." I looked at him questioningly, and he grinned. "You'll see."

He turned and walked down the hall towards the back of the house and I followed him, wondering why we weren't going outside. I followed him into the kitchen and stopped just inside the room and looked around.

The appliances were super old, and a few of the cabinet doors were missing. There was a boarded up window over the chipped farmhouse sink, and a scratched wood table with two chairs. I don't know what I was expecting, but it wasn't this.

Adam headed straight to the fridge and took out a tall glass bottle, filled with dark liquid. I instantly knew it was blood. He set the bottle on the table and turned back to grab two glasses from the cupboard.

I watched him, confused. "You have blood in the fridge?"

He set the glasses on the table next to the bottle, then unscrewed the lid. I inhaled sharply when the scent of blood hit me, and rushed to the table with such speed that I banged into it, knocking both glasses over.

"Whoa!" Adam grabbed the bottle, steadying it. He looked at me and chuckled. "Easy."

My heart was pounding, and my fangs pressed against my lips. With shaking hands, I righted the glasses, and Adam started to pour. He barely filled one glass halfway before I grabbed it and chugged it. I moaned in pleasure as I drank. It was cold, which was weird, but it was good. Adam poured himself a glass and pulled out a chair and sat down before casually taking a sip.

I set my empty glass down and licked my lips, feeling foolish. "Sorry."

"Don't be." He grabbed the bottle and poured some more into my glass. I wanted to snatch it from him and drain it but I forced myself to sit in the other chair and wait.

"Learning to control your hunger takes time," he said, leaning back in his chair. "Years even. You're doing surprisingly well, actually."

"I am?" I picked up my glass with shaking hands and took a sip.

He nodded. "When I was a newborn, I had no control. I fed without thinking, like an animal."

I took another sip, glad that my hands were shaking less now. "How do you have blood in the fridge? Where did it come from? And why did you make me hunt animals when you had this?"

"You had to learn to feed, Sarah, and starting with animals is much safer than starting with humans. *Believe* me."

"Oh." That made sense. I took another sip. "Did you start with animals too?"

He looked down at his glass. "No."

"Did your sire help you?"

Adam was quiet for so long that I wished I could take back my question. "My sire was a monster," he finally said. "And she made me a monster too."

She? I was blown away. I felt jealous, and angry, like I'd been betrayed somehow, which was ridiculous.

Unaware of my inner turmoil, Adam took a deep breath and drained his glass. He set it down with a clunk and grinned at me. "Ready for your surprise?"

I stared at him with wide eyes, my glass of blood forgotten. I didn't know what to say, so I just nodded.

My mind was still whirling as we stood up from the table. *She? His sire was a woman?* I followed Adam out the backdoor and was surprised to see a tangled, overgrown flower garden with a wrought-iron bench in the middle. I glanced at Adam, but he was walking briskly towards a small barn that I hadn't realized was there. I hurried to catch up to him. He swung open the two large doors to reveal an old blue pickup.

"Ta-da!" he said, grinning at me.

I knew I should say something, but my mind was still stuck on the fact that his sire was a woman. *Why did that matter? I'd been with other guys before him. And who's to say he even slept with her? Ugh! Of course he slept with her!*

"Um." I gave him what I hoped was a normal-looking smile. "Are we going somewhere?"

"Yes." He walked back to where I stood frozen in place. "A little dinner, a little dancing." He wrapped his arms around me and dipped his head to kiss me.

The touch of his lips wiped all thought from my mind. I moaned and leaned into him, and I could feel him smile against my lips.

He lifted his head and looked down at me. "Ready?"

Fuck yes I'm ready. Take me now, right here on the ground.
"Alright." He released me and headed for the truck.
Oh.

I walked over to the passenger side and climbed in. Adam turned the key, and the engine roared to life. It was crazy loud for a second, then it quieted.

"Sorry," he said, ruefully. "Old truck. It came with the house."

I laughed, and he reached over and took my hand in his before pulling out of the barn. *Were we really going to hold hands in the car like a couple of high school kids heading out to the movies?* His thumb rubbed across the back of my hand and my heart melted. *Hell yeah we were.* I slid a little closer to him and he shot me a smile.

He drove towards the woods and I saw a break in the trees I hadn't noticed before. It was the old, overgrown driveway. Branches and bushes scraped the sides of the truck as we drove down the drive, and after about half a mile we pulled out onto a normal dirt road.

"So, did you say dinner and dancing?" I asked.

"I did." A smile played on his lips, but his eyes stayed on the road.

"Didn't we just have dinner?"

He glanced at me before looking back at the road. "*That* was just an appetizer. A little something to take the edge off."

"O-*kay*." I didn't know what he had planned, but his hand felt wonderful around mine, and he smelled so damn good, so I decided to just go with it.

A short while later Adam slowed and turned onto another road, although it looked more like a trail than an actual road. As we rounded a corner, I saw a small white car parked on the side of the road and my body tensed.

"It's okay," he said, squeezing my hand. He pulled up behind the car and turned off the truck.

"What's going on?" I stared at the car in front of us. Its back window was half covered with stickers.

"This is an old logging road," he explained, rubbing his thumb over the back of my hand. "There are a few trails that lead up the hill to different spots where people go camping."

There were people in these woods. My heart began to pound.

"You need to learn to drink from a human," he continued. My ears started to ring. "Look at me." Adam took my chin in his hand and gently turned my head towards him.

"I can't," I whispered. "I'm not ready."

"You *are* ready." He cupped my cheek with his hand. "You have more control than any newborn I've ever seen."

"How do you know? You've only seen me with animals!"

"It doesn't matter. Even with animals, newborns go into a frenzy. They completely lose it and tear the poor creature to pieces."

I blinked, glad that I hadn't done that. "But it's only been three nights. Maybe I should stick with animals a while longer."

"This is the perfect opportunity. There are only two people camping here tonight and there's no one else around for miles. If you lose control, there will be no witnesses, and no chance of the authorities finding out. It would probably be weeks before anyone even discovered their bodies."

"What!" I exclaimed, horrified.

He shook his head. "Sorry, that came out wrong."

"I don't want to do this," I told him, but part of me did.

Adam smoothed my hair back from my face. "I'll be with you the whole time. If anything starts to go wrong, I'll take over."

I swallowed. "Don't let me kill anyone."

He smiled. "Never."

CHAPTER 11

I climbed out of the truck and I could instantly smell smoke from the campfire. I followed Adam into the forest, moving swiftly, but silently. It wasn't long before I heard music, and someone laughing. My fangs came down, and I started to rush forward, but Adam wrapped his arms around me and pulled me back against his chest.

"Slowly," he whispered, his lips brushing against my ear. A shiver ran through me and I wanted to turn around and kiss him. "Come on."

He took me by the hand and led me off the trail. We cut through the woods, circling the campsite. We were still a ways back, but I could see them clearly and I could hear every word of their conversation. My vampire senses amazed me.

It was a couple in their early twenties. They were dancing by the campfire, laughing and drinking beer. The guy tipped his head back to drain his beer and when I saw his exposed neck, I tried to run. But again, Adam stopped me. He wrapped his arms around me, pulling me back tightly against his chest.

"Be patient," he whispered against my ear, and I arched against him, sighing with pleasure. "You like that do you?" He chuckled softly, then he pressed his lips to the spot just beneath my ear and *growled.*

I gasped before I could stop myself, and he quickly covered my mouth with his hand. My eyes widened with surprise.

"Shhh," he whispered, before gently biting my earlobe.

I shuddered against him, then froze as he ran his free hand down my stomach. He unfastened my jeans and pushed his hand inside. Since I wasn't wearing underwear, he had immediate access. His fingers brushed over my clit and my body jolted. He moved lower and ran his fingers over my pussy, which was already wet for him.

He growled against my neck again, and my legs almost gave out. He pushed a finger inside of me, then ran it back up over my clit, circling it a few times before dipping lower again. Mercilessly he teased me, all the while his other hand stayed pressed across my mouth, silencing my moans. I rocked against his hand, trying to make him stay on my clit, but he wouldn't. Every time I was close to coming he would leave my clit and push his finger back inside of me. I whimpered and rocked back against him, feeling his erection against my ass.

I closed my eyes. *Fuck, I needed to come.*

"Not yet," he whispered, as if reading my mind. "I will teach you to be patient."

Fuck! I'd get him back for this somehow.

His hand stilled, and I felt his body tense. I opened my eyes and saw the male camper stumbling through the trees towards us. I yanked against Adam's hold and he responded by pushing two fingers deep inside of me. I pushed down on his hand, wanting him deeper, even as I watched the man get closer. He was obviously drunk and had no idea we were there.

"Almost," Adam whispered. Then his hand was gone, and there was nothing but night air against my back.

I looked over my shoulder, but Adam was gone. *Shit!* I spun around to face the camper. He was only a few feet away. *Shit! What should I do?* He was looking at the ground as he walked, but I must have made a sound because he looked up and his eyes widened with surprise.

Suddenly, Adam appeared behind him and in one swift movement grabbed him, tipped his head to the side, and sank his fangs into his neck. The man's eyes closed, then his body slumped.

Adam lifted his head and looked at me. *"Now."*

I leapt forward and sank my fangs into the man's neck, in the same spot Adam had, shuddering at the first taste of his blood. Without stopping, I opened my eyes and saw Adam. We stood face to face on either side of the man. Adam's eyes were completely black, and he had blood smeared across his lips. Suddenly I cared more for those lips than the blood I drank.

I lifted my head and stood up on my toes to press my mouth to Adam's, with the camper's body still pressed between us. Adam's eyes widened in surprise. He pulled back, breaking our kiss, and I frowned. He lowered the man to the ground, crouching beside him. He pressed his thumb to one fang and rubbed it across our bite marks. Then he looked up at me and I saw the hunger in his eyes.

Fuck yes.

He stood up, stepped over the man on the ground, and reached for me. I thought he was going to take me in his arms, but instead he grabbed the top of my jeans with both hands and yanked them down so hard I almost fell over. I barely had time to blink before he spun me around and pressed me against the wide trunk of a tree. I gasped as the rough bark scratched my cheek, then moaned as his cock thrust into me.

He leaned close to my ear. "*Shhh.*" He started to move, and I bit my lip to keep quiet. After all his teasing, my body was ready for him. I was going to come fast, and hard. As if knowing this, he began to pound me furiously, sliding in and out of me with inhuman speed.

I stuffed my hand in my mouth and bit down to keep from screaming as I came. His body stiffened, and I felt his cock pulse inside of me. He thrust a few more times before collapsing against me. I continued to lean against the tree, stunned by what just happened.

Adam pressed a kiss to my neck and pulled out of me. Then he leaned down to grab my pants, which were bunched around my ankles. While he was down there, he pressed a kiss to my bare ass, and I immediately wanted his face between my legs. I had to control my disappointment when he stood back up, pulling my jeans up and fastening them for me. Finally, I turned around to face him.

"I've taught you to be patient," he said. "Now I need to teach you to be quiet." My mouth dropped open, and he grinned. "Let's go."

I looked at the guy on the ground. "Will he be okay?"

"Yeah. He'll come around in a few minutes and probably assume he had too much to drink and passed out for a bit. He won't remember any of this."

Adam took me by the hand and led me back to the truck. He started the engine, then looked at me, his brow furrowed. "You stopped on your own."

I looked at him, confused. "What?"

"When you fed from that guy, you stopped on your own. I didn't have to make you."

"You thought you'd have to make me stop?"

Adam huffed. "Yeah. I thought I was going to have to pry you off of him. What you did-" He shook his head. "It's kind of amazing."

Oh. Well.

He shook his head again before turning the truck around and driving back down the road.

I sat in silence as he drove, pondering my new sex life. Since my mom was terminally ill for my teen years, I never went through the boy-crazy phase most girls go through. As an adult, I had a few flings, but never got close to anyone. Then I met Adam and suddenly I'm a nymphomaniac? *What was it about him?*

We drove for a while before turning onto a paved road. I started to see houses alongside the road, and as we got closer to town, I saw the lights of a shopping center and the giant glowing sign of a Walmart. I tensed when Adam pulled into the turn-only lane.

"Why are we stopping?" I asked.

"You need clothes, among other things." He pulled into a parking spot and turned off the engine.

"This is a bad idea," I said, clenching my hands into fists.

He turned to face me. "You've already fed tonight. Twice, if you count what you drank in the kitchen. So you shouldn't feel the need to feed again. Plus, as I mentioned earlier, you have more self-control than I've ever seen in a newborn. You'll be fine."

"What if I act weird though? People will notice."

Adam laughed. "Have you seen the type of people that shop at Walmart late at night? No one is going to pay any attention to you."

I swallowed nervously. "Okay."

We walked towards the store hand in hand. Inside, Adam grabbed a cart, and we headed to the women's clothing section. I was relieved to see that other than a couple of sleepy-looking cashiers, the store was basically empty.

"They're closing soon," Adam said. "So you don't have time to try a bunch of stuff on. You can always get a couple different sizes and just toss out what doesn't fit."

"Toss out?" I raised my eyebrows at him. "What, vampires don't do returns?"

He gave me a wry look. "We try to limit our trips to the store as much as possible."

"I feel bad wasting your money like that. I feel bad even spending your money in the first place. Come to think of it, how do you even have money? It's not like you have a job, right? Or do you? That's probably something I should've asked before now."

Adam chuckled. "No, I don't have a job. Most vampires don't. We're more into investments. But I'll explain all that tomorrow. Right now we're wasting precious shopping time. You need clothes, and shoes. Don't forget we're going dancing after this. And you'll need toiletries." He shot me a sideways glance. "I'd like my hairbrush back eventually."

I elbowed him in the side. "Okay, you asked for it."

I tossed in jeans, t-shirts, sweatshirts, tank tops, shorts, sundresses, a denim jacket, two purses, several pairs of shoes, socks, and pajamas. In no time at all, the cart was filled to the brim. When we reached the underwear section, I hesitated and looked at Adam.

He lifted a pink lace thong from atop a pile and grinned at me. "Do I get any say in this?"

I swatted his hand, and he dropped the underwear.

"No," I said, fighting a smile. "Go stand over there." I nodded to the end of the aisle.

He sighed dramatically and walked away. He leaned against a shelf, keeping his back to me. I quickly grabbed the pink thong and stuffed it in the cart under a sweatshirt before picking out a bunch of bras and underwear. Once I had a pile of underthings in the cart, I started to cover them with clothes, then I stopped. After everything I'd done with Adam, I was shy about him seeing my underwear?

I headed over to Adam. He glanced in the cart then at me. "Now how about a hairbrush?"

A minute later, I stood in front of the lotion wondering if I even needed it anymore. *Did vampires get dry skin?* I heaved a sigh.

"Problem?" Adam asked over his shoulder. He stood at the end of the aisle, giving me privacy to pick out my "feminine stuff" as he put it.

"No, I'm good." I tossed the lotion in the cart, along with shampoo, conditioner, and deodorant. I stopped in front of the makeup section, then caught sight of myself in a mirror. *Oh yeah, I have flawless, radiant skin now.* No need for makeup then. I'll admit that I was pleased about that.

I stood behind Adam at the checkout and kept my face averted, in case my eyes turned black or my fangs came down. Everything went smoothly though, and we were back at the truck in no time.

Luckily there was a locker box in the back of the truck because there was no way all my clothes would fit in the front with us. I grabbed a sundress and a pair of strappy sandals out of a bag, and helped Adam toss the rest of the stuff in the back. A few minutes later we were back on the road.

I changed into my new dress as Adam drove. He glanced at me a couple times and I scowled at him playfully. "Eyes on the road."

I forgot to grab a bra and underwear so I had nothing on under my dress. *Oh well. Adam would have easy access later on.* I smiled at the thought.

"What's so funny?" he asked.

"Nothing," I said innocently. "I'm just in a good mood."

He glanced at me out of the corner of his eye, and I laughed.

CHAPTER 12

We drove further into town and there were people everywhere. I watched them as we drove past and though I didn't feel an uncontrollable need to feed, I was definitely wound tight. I felt excited and alert.

"This must be how a cat feels, watching birds through the window," I murmured as we drove past a group of people.

Adam parked on the side of the road and came around to open my door. He took my hand as I climbed down and I gripped him tightly. A couple of guys were walking towards us. They were talking and laughing, totally unaware of the danger they were in.

"Look at me," Adam said. I turned away from the men and met Adam's eyes. "Don't make me give you another lesson in patience." He slid his free hand down my hip and grabbed the fabric of my dress in his fist, bunching it up, raising the hem several inches.

I leaned forward and lifted up on my toes to press my lips to his. He deepened our kiss, sliding his tongue into my mouth, and I moaned against him. He stepped closer, pressing me back with his body until I was pinned between him and the side of the truck.

"Yeah buddy! Give it to her!" One guy shouted as they walked by. His friend burst out laughing.

Adam lifted his head and looked down at me. "I intend to, but first we're going dancing."

When we approached the club, it became obvious that I was underdressed. Adam fit in with his navy button-down shirt and dark jeans, but I stood out like a sore thumb in my new sundress. The women waiting to get in were all wearing tight mini dresses with dangerously high heels.

Adam led me to the front of the line, handed the bouncer some cash, and we went straight inside.

We'd been able to hear the music from outside, but inside, with my vampire hearing, it was deafening. I raised my hands to cover my ears, but Adam grabbed them and lowered them, leaning close to speak into my ear.

"Focus your senses," he said, his lips grazing my earlobe. "Focus on my voice and let the rest fall to the background."

I nodded, even though I had no idea how to do that.

He let go of my wrists and placed his hands on my hips. He pressed his body against mine and began to sway to the music.

"You look absolutely delicious in that dress, by the way," he said against my ear. "Later I'm going to bite every one of those little buttons off, and feast on what's underneath."

He began moving, guiding my body backwards until we were in the middle of the dance floor. "I'm going to bury my face between your thighs and finally do what I've been dreaming about ever since I met you." He pressed a thigh between my legs and I rocked against it. His hands grabbed my ass and pulled me tighter.

"I'm going to lick you, *so* slowly, until you beg me to stop." He nipped at my earlobe again and I rocked harder against his thigh. I wrapped my arms around his neck, holding him tight. The noise from the club faded away until it was just us. It was just his voice in my ear, sending shivers of pleasure down my spine.

"I'm going to push my tongue inside of you," he continued, as I rocked against his thigh. "Just for a taste, before I fill you with my cock."

I groaned and closed my eyes. Pressure was building inside of me. *Was I seriously going to come in the middle of the crowded dance floor?*

"That's it, Sarah," he whispered. "Let go."

I rocked against him faster, my hips moving in rhythm with the music. Fuck, I was close already.

"Adam-"

He growled against my neck and my orgasm hit me so hard my legs gave out. He held me up, with his hands still gripping my ass, and rubbed his thigh back and forth against my throbbing pussy.

I gasped, letting my head fall back, then I opened my eyes and looked up at him. His eyes were black but his parted lips revealed no fang. He stepped back just enough to move his thigh from between my legs and slid his hands back up to my waist.

"How are you so in control right now?" I asked, my body still throbbing.

"My control is an illusion," he said. "I'm a breath away from ripping that dress off you and taking you right here."

Oh. Damn.

"Is the noise level okay now?" he asked.

It was. When did that happen? God, he was amazing.

"You're incredible!" I laughed. "I think I lo-" I froze, staring at him with wide eyes. I'd almost said I love you, which was crazy.

Adam stopped moving. He stared at me with such intensity that I couldn't breathe. Then he slowly lowered his head and brushed his lips against mine. It was as though time stopped and we were the only two souls in the universe. He raised his head and looked down into my eyes. Then one corner of his mouth curled up, and he gripped my hand and spun me around so fast that I shrieked. He caught me again and started swaying to the music.

We danced for hours. For *hours* without getting tired, without my feet hurting, or without me having to stand in line for the ladies room. I was beginning to see the perks of being a vampire.

Eventually, Adam told me it was time to go, and we left the club with his arm around me. I was leaning into him, laughing at something he'd said when someone bumped into me.

"Excuse me," the man said.

"No worries," I replied, even as I felt Adam's body go tense. He stopped so suddenly I stumbled. I glanced up at him, but he was staring at the man who'd bumped into me. In fact, they were staring at each other.

"New in town?" The stranger casually asked, his eyes on Adam.

"Just passing through," Adam replied, his face blank.

"You should stay awhile." The stranger turned his gaze to me. "There are many pleasures to be had."

Adam's arm tightened around my waist almost to the point of being painful. My heart was pounding. I didn't know what was happening, but I knew it wasn't good.

"I'd love to show you around," he said, still looking at me.

I looked down, avoiding his gaze.

"I'm afraid we have a prior commitment," Adam said.

"That's a shame," the man said, finally looking back to Adam. They nodded to each other, and the man continued into the club.

I looked up at Adam. "What just happened?"

"I'll explain in the truck," he said tensely. He started walking, pulling me alongside him. He was moving as fast as possible without drawing attention, and I had to jog to keep up. We got back to the truck, and he was peeling away from the curb before I even had my door closed.

"Shit! Adam!" I slammed the door shut and turned sideways on the seat to face him. "What's wrong?" His jaw was clenched, and he had a white knuckle grip on the steering wheel. "Was that a vampire?"

"Yes."

"Are we in trouble?"

"Yes."

I waited for him to continue but he fell silent. "You need to tell me what's happening, Adam, 'cause I'm starting to freak out. Was he part of the Strategoi?"

Adam shook his head. "He knows you're a newborn."

"Which is... bad?"

"Yeah. It's bad. The Strategoi only hears requests for *changes* once a year, at an annual gathering that takes place in November. So right now he's wondering how he just met a newborn in May."

"How could he have known I was a newborn?"

"Newly turned vampires have a distinct smell, half human, half vampire. Over the first few weeks, the human scent gradually wears off until all that's left is vampire."

"Maybe he won't tell anyone," I whispered fearfully.

Adam reached over and took my hand. "He will, Sarah. He'll do it to prove his loyalty to the Strategoi. To earn their favor."

"So what do we do now?"

"We run."

We got home an hour before dawn. It was too late to run. Adam told me we'd have to stay for the day and head out as soon as the sun went down. He sent me up to bed, telling me there were a few things he had to take care of.

I lay in bed, too alert to sleep, jumping at every sound. After a while Adam came in, and I sighed with relief.

"We'll leave as soon as the sun sets," he told me as he took his clothes out of the dresser and stuffed them into a large, black duffle bag. "There's a place in Tennessee. We'll stop for a night, then move on. We need to get as far from here as possible." He zipped the duffle bag and kicked off his shoes before climbing onto the bed fully dressed. I had changed out of my sundress into leggings and a t-shirt. I snuggled close to him and he wrapped his arms around me.

"I promise I won't let anything happen to you," he said, pressing a kiss to the top of my head.

I squeezed my eyes shut, fighting tears. I should never have stayed with Adam. He was in danger because of me. I needed to find a way to leave him, to keep him safe, but I had no idea how to survive on my own. Where would I even go? My apartment was out, since I was getting evicted. Going home to Allie was out of the question. I'd probably end up attacking her. I racked my mind, trying to form a plan, until I eventually drifted off.

CHAPTER 13

I woke to Adam gripping my shoulders. "They're here," he whispered. Before I had a chance to react, the door was kicked in and what looked like a SWAT team burst into the bedroom.

There were six of them, dressed in black tactical gear, with helmets that left only the bottom half of their face visible. They were all armed, and the red lasers from their guns glowed in the darkness. I jerked up-right in bed and Adam shoved me behind him.

"Adam De Clare," one of them spoke, revealing his fangs. "You are to stand before the Strategoi to be judged for your crimes."

"No!" I shouted over Adam's shoulder. "He didn't do anything! This is all a misunderstanding! Tell them Adam!" I looked at him but he remained silent.

Two of them approached the bed, and I shrank back against the headboard.

"Don't struggle," Adam said, his voice grim.

The two guards grabbed us and pulled us off the bed while the others kept their guns on us. They bound our wrists with large, heavy handcuffs that looked like something out of a medieval dungeon.

"Please! Let us explain!" I begged, as they dragged us out of the room. I tripped and stumbled as they pulled me down the hall. When we reached the top of the stairs, I could see more armed vampires standing at the bottom. One of them opened the front door, and the soft rays of the setting sun filled the entryway.

I shrieked and tried to scramble backwards up the stairs, but was shoved forward again. I watched them lead Adam towards the door, and I screamed his name.

"It's alright Sarah," he said, looking over his shoulder at me.

Adam flinched when he stepped into the sun. His jaw clenched, but he remained silent, even as his skin began to redden and flake. Then he was through the door and out of sight.

"Move." The vampire behind me shoved me again, almost making me fall down the stairs.

"No!" I shrieked, grabbing at the railing. "Please! No!"

I screamed when I stepped into the sunlight. The pain was unbearable. I tried to cover my face with my arms, but someone grabbed my bound wrists and yanked me forward. My vision went red, then black. I could see nothing, I was blind. I felt my skin crack as it burned, and I continued to scream as they dragged me along.

It seemed like an eternity, but it was only a few steps until I was thrown into the back of a van. I was still blind, but I could feel the cold metal floor against my cheek. I heard the door slam shut before I lost consciousness.

I came to slowly. The vibration of the moving van was the first thing I noticed, then the hard metal surface beneath me. I opened my eyes, and a sob escaped me when I realized I could see again. Adam was sitting on a metal bench on the other side of the van. His wrists and ankles were shackled to the van with thick metal chains, and his eyes were locked on mine.

I started to push myself up into a sitting position and became aware that I was also chained to the van. Although my chains allowed me some freedom to move, where Adam was locked tight in place.

I whimpered his name, and the muscle in his jaw ticked, but he didn't respond. I looked down at my hands and saw that my skin was smooth and unburnt. *How did that happen?*

Two vampires rode with us, sitting at the back of the van near the doors. They were facing us, but I couldn't see their eyes through the dark visors on their helmets. Each of them held a baton in their lap.

"Where are you taking us?" My voice was rough and scratchy. Neither vampire responded. "This is all a big misunderstanding," I said, clearing my throat.

They continued to ignore me. I glanced at Adam, who was still silently watching me. "He didn't change me," I told them. "We don't know who did. He was just giving me a place to stay. He didn't do anything wrong." No response. "Tell them Adam." He looked at me but said nothing.

"Why won't you say anything?" My voice cracked with emotion. He looked at the guards and one of them smirked. Adam lowered his gaze to stare at the floor.

I stared at him. *Why wouldn't he say anything? Why didn't he try to defend us? I knew we were too outnumbered to fight, but he could at least try to explain our situation! He could at least tell them he was innocent!* I clenched my jaw to hold in my sobs and turned my face away. I leaned against the side of the van, the chains that bound me digging into my skin.

We rode for hours in silence. Eventually the van slowed and turned into what I thought was a driveway or parking lot. The engine cut off and the two guards climbed out of the back, leaving me alone with Adam.

"We're going to stand trial," he said quietly. I looked at him and our eyes met. "It doesn't matter what we've done, only what they *think* we've done. Innocent until proven guilty doesn't exist in our world. I wish I could tell you that everything will be okay, but it won't. They will sentence us both to death."

I felt a tear roll down my cheek, and I strained against my chains trying to get closer to him. *"Adam."*

"I'm sorry, Sarah," he said, his eyes rimming with unshed tears. "I'm *so* sorry."

Four guards appeared at the back of the van and trained their lasers on us. A fifth climbed inside and unhooked us from the benches, leaving our hands cuffed in front of us.

"Out," he said, his voice cold.

I watched Adam stand and climb out of the van, then the guard turned to me. I stood on wobbly legs and climbed out of the van. I started to fall and one of the other guards grabbed my arm and jerked me upright. I looked around and saw we were in an underground parking garage. There were a few black vans like the one we just climbed out of, a row of military Humvee looking vehicles, and two rows of luxury cars.

"Where are we?" I asked.

Instead of replying, the guard at my side yanked on my arm, pulling me away from the group. "Come."

I looked back at Adam and saw the rest of the guards were ushering him in a different direction. I tried to turn back towards him but the guard beside me yanked me hard.

"Adam!" I screamed, struggling against the vampire holding me.

"Don't fight them Sarah!" Adam shouted, but his warning came too late. The guard slammed a metal baton into my stomach, sending an electrical current through my body. I couldn't even scream. I was paralyzed as my body shook. Then it was over and I collapsed onto the cement, blood running out of my nose.

My captor grabbed the chain binding my wrists and dragged me across the floor to the elevator. My ears were ringing loudly but I could hear Adam shouting my name before I blacked out.

CHAPTER 14

The next time I woke I was alone in a cement room containing nothing but the cot I lay on. Thankfully, my shackles were gone. I sat up and looked around. There were no windows, only a steel door on one wall with a narrow slot near the top. I jumped up, rushed to the door and pounded my fists against it.

"Open the door! I want to see Adam!" My cries echoed in the room. "Let me out of here!" Eventually I wore myself out and returned to the cot. A moment later, the slot at the top of the door slid open, and a bag of blood was pushed through before the slot slammed closed again. I rushed to the door and pounded again. "Come back!"

I looked at the bag on the floor. It looked like the kind hospitals used when you donated blood. I wondered briefly if it was poisoned, then my hunger took over and I tore the cap off and drained the bag.

I don't know how long they kept me there. I slept on and off, and a bag of blood was dropped in two more times.

I was asleep when they came the fourth time. I heard a noise at the door and opened my eyes, expecting to see a bag drop through the slot. Instead, the door swung open and an armed guard stepped in.

I lept off the bed and bared my fangs at him, a feral hiss escaping me. I didn't have a chance to ponder the sound I'd just made, because a second guard entered the room holding a metal baton at his side, the tip crackling with electricity. I froze, and the guard's lips curled into a sinister smile.

"Come," the first guard said, stepping to the side to allow me to exit the room. I passed him cautiously, afraid he might strike me. The guard with the baton led the way, and I stared at the crackling tip as I followed, the second guard falling into place behind me. We walked down a long hallway lined on both sides with steel doors like the one on my cell. *Was Adam in one of those rooms?*

They led me up a flight of stairs to what appeared to be the main floor. They took me down several hallways, turning this way and that, passing countless closed doors along the way. These doors were made of wood, and the floor I walked on looked like polished marble.

We rounded another corner, and I saw two guards standing in front of a closed door. As we approached, they stepped to the side, allowing us to pass. The guard in front of me pushed open the large door, and I followed him through, stumbling to a halt when I saw the room.

"Walk." The guard behind me shoved me, and I stumbled forward. My eyes darted around the room as I walked, taking in every detail.

It was an enormous space, with soaring ceilings and tall stone pillars in the corners. At the end of the room was a raised platform, like a stage, with eight large wooden chairs that looked like thrones. Three of them were occupied by lavishly dressed vampires, a woman in the middle, and a man seated on either side.

A crowd of vampires stood to the side of the room and several of them bared their fangs at me as I passed. They were all dressed elegantly, as if this were an upscale cocktail party rather than a trial.

The guard in front of me came to a stop just before the raised platform. "Here," he said, pointing to a spot on the floor with his baton.

I stepped forward and looked up at the three vampires seated before me. They stared down at me, their faces void of emotion.

A commotion broke out behind me and I turned to see Adam being led into the room, still shackled at the wrists and ankles. The length of chain between his ankles only allowed him to take small steps, and the vampires in the crowd hissed and cursed him as he passed. Our eyes met, and he held my gaze as he crossed the room to stand beside me.

I tried to step towards him, but the guard beside me yanked me back into place. I wondered why Adam was still shackled when I was free.

"Adam De Clare, formerly of House Velasco." The female vampire on the stage spoke, and Adam and I both turned to face her. She was wearing a black gown that pooled at her feet.

Her dark hair was twisted high atop her head, and she had diamonds at her neck and ears. "You are here to be judged for the crimes of hericide and unauthorized creation. Do you deny these charges?" Her voice rang out in the now silent room.

Adam raised his chin. "No."

What? My eyes darted back and forth between Adam and the female vampire. "Adam," I began, and the woman's eyes shot to me. I flinched under her gaze, but refused to be silent. "Adam, tell them the truth." I looked sideways at him but he stared straight ahead. "He didn't turn me," I said, looking up at the woman. "He didn't do any of those things. Another vampire turned me, I don't know who it was, but Adam found me and was helping me. He was teaching me about vampire rules, so I didn't get noticed by humans. He was trying to do the right thing. We both were!" I looked at Adam again. *Why was he just standing there? Why wouldn't he defend himself?* "Adam!" I practically screamed his name, and he flinched.

"Does she truly not know?" The woman directed the question at Adam.

He glanced at me then, his face tense. "She is completely innocent in all of this," he said, looking back to the three on the stage. "I ask that the Strategoi take her innocence into consideration and allow her a quick death."

What? My jaw dropped. *Was Adam asking them to kill me?*

The three vampires exchanged a look before the female spoke again. "Is that truly what you wish, when her life could be spared through *metapherus archond*?" I heard gasps and murmurs from the crowd.

"Yes," Adam replied, staring straight ahead.

"What the fuck Adam!" I screeched, but he continued to stare blankly ahead. I turned to the female. "Hey!" I shouted, getting her attention. "Will you please explain what the *fuck* is going on? Because I haven't done anything wrong, and I don't want to die."

The woman stared down at me. "She has fire." I waited for her to continue, but instead she looked over my head to address the crowd. "Is there anyone here who will accept this newborn?"

"*What?*" My eyes darted around the room. "What does that mean?" No one paid any attention to me.

"I will." A voice rang out from the back of the room.

I started to turn to see who had spoken, but was startled when Adam's roar filled the room. He spun around, mindless of his chains, and lunged towards the crowd at the back of the room.

A guard rushed forward and jammed a baton into Adam's back. His body jerked as electricity coursed through him, but he grabbed the end of the baton and yanked hard, sending the guard on the other end careening toward him. Adam lifted the guard and threw him across the room, just as two others rushed in. I watched in disbelief as Adam fought them both at once. Even with him chained, they didn't stand a chance. He tore into them with his fangs and his claws.

The vampires in the room were all shouting, but I couldn't take my eyes off Adam. He fought like an animal. *Where had this strength been when we were captured?*

An arm came sliding across the floor towards me. *Just* an arm. I slapped a hand over my mouth and jumped back as blood came pooling towards my feet.

The female on the stage was shouting, and four more guards joined the fray. They hit him with electric batons, over and over, eventually bringing him to his knees, and still they did not stop.

I tried to run to him, but the guard at my side grabbed me and held me in place. I screamed Adam's name and struggled to get free, but I wasn't strong enough.

"Enough!" The female on the stage shouted, rising to her feet. The four remaining guards lowered their batons and stepped away. Adam lay unmoving on the floor, his eyes closed. *Was he alive? He had to be!* Three dead bodies lay on the floor around him, one of them in multiple pieces.

"Adam-" I choked, hot tears running down my face.

"Well, *that* was unexpected," a man said dryly. I turned and saw a vampire crossing the room towards me. He was massive, taller than Adam even, with dark hair and olive tanned skin. He was wearing a black suit, and I stared at his polished shoes as he casually stepped over a dead guard on his way towards me.

"Julian Calahorra of House Velasco." I heard the woman say. "Do you accept this newborn through metapherus archond?"

"Yes." The man came to a stop a foot in front of me. I had to tilt my head back to see his face. He looked down at me, his dark eyes fathomless. I wanted to run, but my feet wouldn't

move. I was like a mouse caught in a snake's stare. "I accept."
He said, looking directly into my eyes as he spoke.

"Then it is done." I heard the woman say.

"What is done?" I asked, still unable to look away from him.
"What does that mean?"

His full lips slowly curved into a cruel smile. "It means you
belong to me now."

PART TWO

BOUND BY DARKNESS

CHAPTER 15

*Y*ou belong to me now.

The vampire's words echoed in my mind as all other sounds faded away. The world around me began to spin, and I prayed I wouldn't pass out. His dark eyes held mine, and I was trapped, unable to look away. Finally he turned away to address another, and I quickly looked back to Adam. He still lay unmoving on the floor, surrounded by the guards who had beaten him. *Please be alive!* I stared at him, willing him to open his eyes.

Two guards approached me and I became aware that the other vampire was looking at me again. *Julian.*

"What's happening?" I cried, stepping away from the guards. My eyes darted from the guards, to Julian, to Adam. One guard grabbed my arm roughly. "Don't touch me!" I shrieked, yanking free of him.

I scrambled backwards, frantically looking for an escape route. I saw the guard reach for the electric baton hanging at his side and my eyes widened. *God no.* He smiled at my obvious fear as he pulled the baton free. I blinked, and Julian was there, holding the man's heart in his fist. I watched in slow motion as the guard crumpled to the ground, his cruel smile still frozen on his lips.

"Let this be a reminder," Julian said loudly, holding the bloody heart high for all to see. "You do not touch what is mine." He opened his fist and let the heart fall. It hit the stone floor with a sickening splat. I watched as he pulled a pocket square from his suit jacket and casually wiped the blood from his hand.

He nodded at the remaining guard at my side. "Take her to my room." He looked at me then, as if daring me to resist, but I knew there would be no fighting this man.

A short while later I stood alone in Julian's room, too stunned by everything that had happened to acknowledge my luxurious surroundings. The guard that led me there hadn't spoken at all, and had never moved to touch me. I assumed that after witnessing his coworkers gruesome death he was as frightened as I was. Or maybe he was angry. Maybe the other guard was his friend, and he blamed me for his death?

I shook my head. *Why was I thinking about that? What did the guard's feelings matter when Adam could be dead!*

I sat down on the edge of the bed. *Oh Adam.* I sniffed, watching a red tear land on the back of my hand.

The door swung open, and I leapt to my feet as a middle-aged woman entered the room. She was a few inches shorter than me, with tanned skin and dark brown hair that was twisted up in a tight bun. She wore black slacks and a dark blue blouse that was buttoned all the way up. A small gold cross hung on a dainty chain around her neck. She stopped short when she saw me, her eyes widening.

"Goodness!" she exclaimed, looking me over from head to toe. "We've got to get you cleaned up!"

What?

I watched as she closed the bedroom door and walked briskly across the room, disappearing through another doorway.

"Come along then," she called, from the other room.

Confused, I followed her into what turned out to be a bathroom. The woman was turning on the water in the large glass shower as I entered the room.

"Well, come on." She stepped back from the shower and waved a hand towards me. "Get undressed. We haven't got all night."

"I don't understand what's happening," I mumbled, still in shock.

"I'm Maria. Julian has sent me to prepare you for your journey."

"What journey?"

"Your journey home, to his estate."

He was taking me to his house! I had to escape now!

"Please!" I begged her. "You have to help me!"

She rolled her eyes. "You can save your pleas for Julian. I'm just here to get you cleaned up."

"But-"

"But nothing. Have you seen yourself?" She waved a hand towards the mirror over the double sinks.

I glanced over and flinched at the sight of myself. My face was caked with dried blood from my tears, and the front of my shirt was torn, revealing half of my bra.

"Now hop in," she said over her shoulder as she exited the room. "I'll go find you some clean clothes."

It felt strange, doing something as ordinary as showering, after what I'd just endured. But I couldn't bear the sight of my face covered in blood. I undressed quickly and jumped in the shower. I faced the door while I scrubbed at my skin, not wanting to be caught unawares.

Maria still hadn't returned when I turned off the shower, so I dried off quickly and grabbed a fluffy white robe off a hook by the door. I shoved my arms into it and cinched it tightly around my waist before heading back into the bedroom.

The room was empty. I looked at the door and wondered if it was unlocked. Not that it mattered. I wasn't about to wander around a house full of vampires wearing nothing but a bathrobe. I walked over to the large windows and looked out. I was on the second floor, overlooking a large circular driveway with endless manicured lawns stretching into the distance. A dozen guards stood in the driveway.

"I hope you're not thinking about jumping."

I spun around at the sound of a voice behind me and saw Julian standing at the foot of the bed. I took a step back, bumping against the window.

My heart hammered as he crossed the room towards me. He came to a stop directly in front of me, and I pressed myself back against the window until I feared the glass would break. I stared straight ahead, my eyes level with his chest, until he took my chin in his hand and lifted my face. Our eyes met, and I quickly looked away, not wanting to be caught in his hypnotic stare again. Instead, I focused on his mouth as he spoke.

"You have piqued my curiosity," he said softly. "For two hundred years Adam has safely hidden himself away. He knew discovery would lead to his death, and yet he took that risk for you." His eyes narrowed a fraction. "Why? What's so special about *you*?"

I was too terrified to respond.

"*Sa-rah.*" He drew my name out, rubbing his thumb across my lips as he spoke.

Without thinking I bit him, hard. I instantly regretted my foolishness, but he only laughed. I watched him raise his thumb to his lips and slowly lick the blood from it. Then he stepped away, and I let out a shaky breath. He crossed the room and sat down on a loveseat in front of the fireplace.

"Join me," he said, motioning to the chair across from him.

I stared at him, his large frame sprawled so casually on that dainty little couch. It appeared almost comical, but I knew the danger that lurked there.

He sighed loudly. "It's been a long night and my patience wears thin."

I pushed myself away from the window and slowly walked towards him, the hem of my robe brushing the tops of my feet. I nervously perched on the edge of the chair, and my robe parted as I sat down, exposing my bare legs. He looked at my legs and I quickly yanked the robe closed.

"I have questions," he began, "and as I said, it's been a long night, so I'll get right to it. How did you wind up with Adam?"

I hesitated, unsure of how much to reveal. If I spoke the truth, would it help my case or hurt it?

His eyes narrowed. "Speak the truth. Lies will only anger me."

I looked down at my hands in my lap and began nervously twisting the tie to my robe. "I met Adam a few nights ago. I'm not sure- how long I've been here." I shook my head. "I was in the park, and I just killed a man." I glanced at him to see his reaction but he simply watched me, waiting for me to continue.

"So, yeah, I killed a guy," I continued, "and a woman saw it and she wouldn't stop screaming. Then Adam appeared out of nowhere and grabbed me and flew us out of there." I glanced at him nervously, then back at my lap. "He took me to his house and told me about vampires and their rules and how I was in danger for being illegally turned. He said I could stay with him a while, and he'd teach me how to survive. I was scared and alone, and he offered to help." I looked at Julian then, desperate for him to believe me. "Adam offered to help me, a complete stranger, even though it put him at risk. He shouldn't be punished for that! We have to help him!"

Julian stared at me. "You can't truly be this naive."

"I-" *What?*

He rubbed a hand over his face and sighed wearily. "Adam is the one who changed you. His meeting you in the park was a farce."

I shook my head. "That's not true. Adam-"

"Adam is a liar," he said, cutting me off. "And a murder."

"You're lying," I said angrily.

"I never lie, Sarah, know that about me." His voice was sharp, causing me to hesitate and reel in my anger. I was so caught up in my emotions over Adam, I'd momentarily forgotten to be afraid of this man, who had just ripped the beating heart out of someone.

"I'm sorry," I said quickly, looking down at my lap again. "But Adam-"

Julian cut me off again. "Adam killed his sire with a brutality that shook the entire vampire world. He's been in hiding ever since, so you can see why I'm surprised to find him playing house with you."

"I don't believe you," I said, without looking up.

"Look at me," he snapped. I raised my head and our eyes met. "Adam took your life, without your consent. Then he left you to go through the transformation alone. Something that must have been terrifying for you. It's *his* fault you killed that man, and it's *his* fault you're here now."

He stood, and I shrank back in my chair. For a moment he just stood there, looking down at me. Then he turned and walked out of the room, closing the door firmly behind him.

I sat there, not knowing what to think. Why did everyone here think Adam changed me? Adam *saved* me. He cared for me. Didn't he?

I pondered the question until fatigue overtook me. I tried to fight it, but my internal clock was telling me that sunrise was approaching. I moved to the bed and lay down on top of the covers. I fought to keep my eyes open, drifting in and out of sleep. At one point I opened my eyes and saw Julian standing beside the bed, looking down at me. But no, It must have been a dream. I let my eyes close once more.

CHAPTER 16

"Wake up," Maria said, shaking my shoulder. My eyes flew open, and she released me. "Julian will be here shortly, and he wants you dressed and ready." I sat up in bed and pushed my hair out of my face. "Come on now. Unless you want him to catch you dressing." She shot me a suggestive look that had me leaping out of bed.

"Hmph." She shrugged her shoulders. "Your clothes are in the bathroom. I suggest you hurry. Julian is in a mood tonight..."

She didn't finish her thought, and I took it as a bad sign. I rushed into the bathroom and saw a sheer red slip hanging there for me.

"Uh, I don't think so!" I shouted.

A second later Maria poked her head through the doorway.

"Are you serious with this?" I asked, flicking the flimsy material with my hand.

"I'm afraid Julian insists." She frowned, and I felt a flare of hope. *Did she disagree with how Julian was treating me? Could I convince her to help me?*

"Why would he want me to wear something like this?" I didn't have to fake the fear in my voice, though I might have laid it on a little thick for her benefit. "I'm scared, Maria."

Her face softened. "There's no reason to be scared. Julian is better than most of this lot, believe me. The sooner we leave this place the better. And we're not leaving until you get dressed." She glanced at the slip again, then disappeared into the bedroom.

"I refuse to wear this!" I shouted, but she didn't respond. With a huff I leaned against the counter and glared at the slip. No way in hell was I putting that on. Minutes passed, and I eventually sat down on the edge of the tub. *Okay, so what was my plan? Was I going to hide in the bathroom all night?*

I heard the bedroom door slam, and I scrambled to my feet just as Julian stormed into the bathroom. His eyes met mine, and I swallowed at the fury I saw there.

"Put on the damn dress," he ground out.

Despite my fear, I raised my chin. "No."

He crossed the room in two steps, grabbed the shoulders of my robe and ripped it from my body. I gasped as the robe was torn in two and tossed to the floor, and fought the urge to cover myself. Julian glanced down at my body, then his eyes went back to mine. I felt my nipples harden and prayed he wouldn't look down again.

"Then you will wear nothing," he said quietly, before turning and walking out of the room.

I listened for the sound of the bedroom door, to indicate he was leaving, but it never came. I looked at the slip, because it definitely *was* a slip, not a dress, and goosebumps broke out all over my body. I briefly considered wrapping myself in a towel, but didn't want to anger Julian further. Defeated, I put it on.

It had spaghetti straps and came down to my knees. The fabric was blood red, and so sheer you could see every detail of my body beneath. I was given no undergarments.

I took a deep breath to brace myself before going back into the bedroom. Julian was standing at the window with his back to me. I imagined rushing at him and shoving him through the glass, hopefully to his death, then I frowned at my stupidity. A second story fall wouldn't kill a vampire, it would only make him mad.

He turned to face me and I saw he was holding a black leather belt in one hand. His eyes roamed over me. "*Perfect.*"

He walked towards me, and though I wanted to retreat, I forced myself to stand still. He came to a stop directly in front of me and lifted the belt. I jerked back, afraid he was about to strike me.

"Hold still." His voice was firm. I was shaking as he lifted the belt again, and that's when I realized it wasn't a belt at all. It was a thick leather collar, with a metal ring in the front.

My eyes shot to his and his lips curled into a truly terrifying smile. My shaking intensified as he fastened the collar around my throat. I swallowed. It felt too tight. I reached up to grab it but he pushed my hands away. He attached a long slender leash to the ring and took a few steps back, holding the end of the leash in his fist.

I was terrified. And furious. My breath was coming in harsh bursts, causing my chest to rise and fall dramatically.

He tugged on the leash, causing me to stumble towards him. "Come, pet."

I glared at him through tear-filled eyes. "I hate you."

The corner of his mouth curled. "Good."

CHAPTER 17

Julian led me through the house like a dog on a leash. Barefoot, with every inch of my body on display. The few times we encountered someone they stepped aside and bowed their heads as we passed by. The house was enormous, and I was hopelessly lost, until we came to the staircase leading down to the basement where I had been kept before.

"No!" I cried, digging my feet into the stone floor. I grabbed the leash with both hands and pulled, but I might as well have been trying to move a mountain.

"Stop," Julian said harshly, yanking on the leash. My neck cracked as I stumbled forward, nearly colliding with him.

"Come." He turned and started walking down the stairs.

"Please!" I begged, stumbling down the steps behind him. "Don't lock me in here again!"

He led me down the hall of steel doors. Two guards were standing at the end, in front of a cell that was enclosed with thick metal bars, rather than a door.

"Open the door and leave us," Julian told them, as we approached. One guard quickly unlocked the cell door, and they both disappeared down the hall.

I struggled as he pulled me closer to the cell. "Please don't!"

"Sarah?" The voice was faint and raspy, but it was Adam's.

I rushed towards the opening, just getting a glimpse of Adam before Julian yanked on the leash, pulling me back.

"Sarah!" Adam shouted.

Julian casually strolled over to stand in front of the cell, taking me with him, and I could finally see Adam clearly.

"Adam!" I cried out at the sight of him. He was leaning against the far wall of the cell, bound at the wrists and ankles by thick chains that were attached to the wall. His shirt was gone, and his torso was covered in welts and cuts, crusted with dried blood.

"Adam!" I cried again, as hot tears rolled down my face. I pulled at the leash, stretching my arms towards him.

His body was slumped as far as the chains would allow, and he squeezed his eyes shut for a moment before opening them again, as if he was having a hard time focusing. Then his expression cleared and his face hardened. I knew he was taking in my revealing dress and the collar around my neck. He pushed himself upright, still leaning heavily against the wall.

He looked past me to Julian. "I'll kill you for this."

Instead of responding Julian yanked on the leash, causing me to stumble backwards. I yelped, more from shock than pain, and Adam surged forward. He pulled at his chains, causing his muscles to flex, and fresh blood trickled from his wounds.

"Let her go!" he snarled.

Julian gave the leash another little tug. "Not until I've had my fun."

"Why aren't you healing?" I cried, looking at the blood running down Adam's chest.

His body slumped, and he leaned back against the wall again. His eyes met mine. "I'm alright."

"They're starving him," Julian said casually. "He can't heal unless he feeds."

I sobbed and tried to reach for him again, but Julian yanked the leash. Snarling, I spun around to scratch his eyes out. He moved so fast I didn't even see it. He grabbed my face with one hand, gripping painfully.

"Let her go!" Adam roared.

Julian held my face close to his. "I'll enjoy breaking this one."

"You have me, Julian, let her go." Adam's voice broke as he spoke. "Please. I'll do anything. Just let her go."

Julian released my face, and I scrambled as far away as the leash would allow. He looked at Adam for a moment, as if considering his words. "Relinquish control to me, and perhaps I'll be merciful."

"Never!" Adam snarled, yanking on his chains again.

"Relinquish control, or what was done to Valentina will be done to her."

Adam made a choking sound and bowed his head. For a moment everyone was silent. The only sound was my own ragged breathing. Then, Adam lifted his head and looked directly at Julian. "Promise you won't hurt her and I'll relinquish control."

"I promise," Julian agreed.

What was happening? My eyes darted back and forth between them. Whatever they were talking about, Julian agreed far too quickly for me to believe him.

Adam's eyes bore into Julian. "You never lie. Remember that."

Julian nodded once and stepped towards the cell. "Come," he said, without looking at me. Not having any choice, I followed him into the cell. I had no idea what was happening, and I was terrified he was about to kill Adam.

My eyes darted around, looking for a weapon, but of course there were none. *Fine, then I'll jump on his back and tear his throat out.* Just as I was preparing to leap, Julian looked over his shoulder at me.

"Come," he said again. I reluctantly stepped closer, and he grabbed my wrist tugging me to him. He released the leash and lifted his hands to remove my collar.

"What are you going to do?" My voice wavered as I spoke.

"It's okay Sarah," Adam whispered.

As soon as the collar was gone, I threw myself at Adam. I wrapped my arms around his neck and pressed myself against his chest. To my surprise Julian allowed it. Then I felt his body at my back, pressing me harder against Adam. I gasped in shock as my body was pinned between the two of them.

"What are you-" I shrieked as Adam sank his fangs into the side of my neck. "Stop!" I tried to yank away, but Julian pressed me closer, holding my body still. *Why was Adam doing this? And why was Julian helping?*

I tried to struggle, but feelings of pleasure quickly overrode my fear. "*Stop.*" The word came out as a sigh this time, and my eyelids fluttered shut. Involuntarily, my body relaxed, melting against Adam. Arousal began to curl low in my belly, and I hated myself for it. *How could I feel this way when Adam was chained to the wall, beaten and bleeding, and Julian, whom I despised, was pressed against my backside?*

I tried again to tell Adam to stop again, but the words would not come out. Instead, I rubbed myself against him. My slip was so thin it felt like there was nothing between us, and I loved it. I felt my legs give out, but Julian wedged his thigh between my legs, holding me up.

I writhed and moaned as Adam's lips sucked the blood from my body. It seemed to go on forever, and I never wanted it to stop. I started to feel lightheaded, and the thought flitted through my mind that Adam was taking too much. Then I was lost to my pleasure once more. My ears began to ring, and I struggled to open my eyes. The world around me had faded into shadows. There was nothing, except the three of us. *Three? Why were there three of us? That was strange, wasn't it?*

I tried to focus, but my thoughts were fuzzy. My head fell back against Julian's chest, but still Adam didn't stop. Something inside of me knew he should. I looked up and saw Julian looking down at me. His eyes were completely black and his fangs were exposed. *Was he going to drink too? Were they going to kill me?*

I watched Julian raise his wrist to his mouth and bite himself. *No, that couldn't be right. Was I hallucinating?* I could smell the tang of his blood. It was sharp and spicy, and I wanted it. I struggled to focus as he brought his wrist to my mouth. I drank greedily, moaning at the taste of him.

Strength slowly returned to my body. Feeling returned to my legs, and I knew I could stand if I wanted. Instead, I chose to remain held up by Julian. I tried not to give that too much thought. I could feel Julian's blood pumping through my veins, mixing with my own.

Adam lifted his head, pulling his fangs from my neck, but I hardly noticed. I grabbed Julian's wrist with both hands, clasping it against my mouth as I drank. I moaned loudly and rubbed myself against his thigh. He stiffened and stepped back, pulling his wrist away from me. I spun around, desperate for more.

"No." He stepped back, pressing his other hand to his bleeding wrist. "You've had enough."

Desire clouded my mind, and I shook my head, trying to clear it. My body was throbbing with arousal, and I felt desperate for release, but fear slowly began to creep in. *What just happened?* I looked at Adam, still chained to the wall, his mouth smeared with my blood. Then I turned to Julian, who looked smug and satisfied. Warning bells went off in my head.

"Why did you do that?" I asked, not sure which of them I'm talking to.

"You belong to me now," Julian said. "Truly."

"I don't understand." I looked at Adam and was astonished to see his wounds heal in real time.

"Adam!" I cried, throwing myself at him. I hugged him and kissed his face. "You're healing!"

He didn't kiss me back. "I'm sorry," he murmured, bowing his head to rest against mine.

"It's okay," I assured him. "We'll get out of this somehow, now that you're healing."

He shook his head. "I'm sorry, Sarah. I'm so sorry."

I leaned back to look at him, and his expression filled me with dread.

"Touching," Julian said mockingly from behind me. "But it's time to go. *Come, Sarah.*"

I felt his words, like a whip against my skin. My body stiffened and my eyes widened with shock. I whispered Adam's name, even as my hands released him. I tried to stay with him, but my body moved as if someone else was controlling it, my feet carrying me towards Julian.

"Adam," I whispered, terrified by what was happening to me.

"I'm sorry!" he shouted.

My body came to a stop in front of Julian. He raised a hand to touch me, letting his fingertips brush across my collarbone. I was trembling with fear, but unable to move away.

"You know, on second thought," Julian said. "I think I'll continue with my original plan. What was done to Valentina *will* be done to Sarah. *After* I've had my fun that is."

Adam roared and yanked against his chains. "I'll kill you!" The concrete wall cracked where the chains were attached. "Julian! You promised! You never lie!" He yanked again and one chain came bursting free from the wall, showering the cell with bits of concrete.

Fully healed by my blood, those chains were no match for him. Julian seemed to realize that, because he reached past me to slide the cell door closed, locking it.

Adam's shoulder's sank when the door slammed shut. "You gave your word, Julian!" he panted, his chest heaving from exertion, and rage.

"Yes," Julian agreed. "And I never lie. *I* will not harm Sarah. I will use her beautiful body until I tire of it, then I'll turn her over to the Strategoi."

Adam roared again and yanked his other hand free. "I'll kill you!" He pulled at the chains on his ankles.

Unperturbed, Julian brushed his hand across my shoulder, causing the strap of my slip to fall. The flimsy material sagged in the front, exposing one of my breasts. I gasped and tried to yank it back up, but Julian grabbed my wrist, stopping me. Adam raged against his chains, and tears welled in my eyes.

"I hate you!" I cried, choking on a sob.

"Good." He smiled cruelly before releasing me. I yanked my strap up and rushed to the cell. I reached between the bars, trying to get to Adam.

He stopped fighting his chains, and his shoulders slumped in defeat. "I'm so sorry, Sarah."

Julian turned and started walking away. *"Come, Sarah."*

I once again lost control of my body. I screamed Adam's name as my body turned and walked away from him.

Adam shouted my name, until we exited the dungeon and Julian closed the door, cutting off his voice. He glanced at me briefly, then turned and walked back up to his room. There was nothing I could do but follow.

CHAPTER 18

When we got back to Julian's room Maria was there waiting.

"Get her cleaned up," Julian said to her. "We leave in thirty minutes." Then he left, closing the door behind him.

I stood there, staring at Maria, too overwrought to say anything.

She gave me a sympathetic look. "Go wash your face. There are clean clothes in the bathroom."

Numbly, I walked to the bathroom. I glanced at myself in the mirror, and once again, I was covered in blood. My face from my tears, and my chin and neck from the feeding that took place in the dungeon. Whatever *that* was, it had somehow given Julian power over me. I prayed there was a way to reverse it.

In a daze, I washed and dressed in the clothes that were laid out for me. Black leggings, a silk camisole, and an over-sized sweater. I slipped my feet into the black flats that were provided, still in too much shock to notice that everything fit perfectly.

Maria was still waiting in the bedroom. I followed her downstairs, and this time we didn't encounter anyone else. We exited the building, and I shivered when the night air touched my skin. After being locked in that house for so long, being outside felt wonderful. It was strange to notice something pleasant like that after everything I'd just been through.

We started to descend a large stone staircase, and that's when I noticed the helicopter. Julian stood beside it, talking to another man. *He was taking me away from Adam*. My steps faltered, and his head snapped towards me. Even from this distance I could feel his dark eyes on me. I continued down the steps and followed Maria across the lawn.

The helicopter ride was unpleasant, to say the least. Neither Julian nor Maria spoke as we flew. The sound was deafening, even with the protective headphones I wore. I tried to focus my senses, like Adam taught me, but I was too upset.

We landed on a runway beside a private jet, and in a matter of minutes I found myself back in the air, seated in a plush leather chair across from Julian. Maria had disappeared into a room at the back of the plane, leaving the two of us alone. Julian watched me silently, and I looked down at my lap, avoiding his gaze.

"We're flying to Madrid, in case you're wondering," he said, finally breaking the silence.

My eyes shot to his. "Why?"

"That's where I live. Therefore, that's where you live now."

"You want me to *live* with you?" I didn't bother hiding my distaste.

"It's what's expected."

By who? "What did you do to me earlier?"

"Adam relinquished his control over you to me."

I shook my head. "I don't understand. How did you make me follow you like that?"

He sighed and looked at me in a way that suggested I should already know the answer. "A sire can call their progeny to them. Adam had that power, and now he has given it to me."

I frowned. "Adam didn't have that power."

"Yes, he did. He didn't use it because he didn't want you to know he was the one who changed you."

"I don't believe you."

He tilted his head as he looked at me. "I think you do."

I looked away. *Did I?* Whatever went on in that cell, Adam had taken part willingly. I swallowed at the lump in my throat and curled my hands into fists, digging my nails into my palms. *I would not cry in front of him.*

I took several deep breaths to calm myself before I trusted myself to speak. "Who is Valentina, and what happened to her?"

A muscle in his jaw twitched. "Valentina is none of your concern. But you needn't be afraid, I have no intentions of harming you."

"Then why did you say those things to Adam?"

"Because I wanted his last hours to be filled with sorrow and fear for you."

His last hours? "What's going to happen to him?"

"He's going to be executed. Tonight, probably."

I screamed and flew at him, but he caught me easily. He pushed me back into my seat, looming over me.

"Do not test me," he snarled, his face inches from mine. "I have no intentions of hurting you, but there are other ways to assert my control over you." He lowered his face, and I turned away. He pressed his face to my neck and inhaled deeply. I squeezed my eyes shut, bracing for his bite. But it never came. He released me, and I cautiously opened my eyes to see him back in his own chair, his completely black eyes the only sign that I hadn't imagined the whole thing.

We arrived in Spain just before sunrise. We climbed into the back of a limo that had special windows to block out the sun, making it impossible for me to see outside. I wondered how the driver was surviving on the other side of the partition, but I didn't ask.

When we arrived at Julian's home, we exited the car into an underground garage. Julian told Maria to take me to my room and promptly walked away.

I followed her through the house, which was even larger and more luxurious than the last place. We passed many windows, but all I could see through the glass was what looked like dark gray metal.

"Steel shutters protect us during daylight hours," Maria explained, noticing my stare.

I followed her up a large curved staircase and down a long hall. We eventually came to a door which led to the most beautiful suit of rooms imaginable.

"This is you." She stepped aside, allowing me to enter the room. She followed me in, and I noticed she didn't bother closing the door behind her. I tried not to stare at the doorway as she told me about the room. *Closet through here, bathroom through there. Yeah, yeah. Was my door going to remain unlocked? Could I possibly escape?*

"And of course, the shutters will automatically open after sundown," Maria said, motioning to the wall of windows on the far side of the room. "You have a lovely view from this room."

I nodded, as if I'd been paying attention all along.

I planned on escaping as soon as she left, but my internal clock had other ideas. I barely made it to the bed before I passed out. *How was Maria still so wide awake?* I wondered, before slipping fully into sleep.

CHAPTER 19

A noise woke me, like the soft click of a door closing. My eyes shot open, but I was alone in the room. It had been the shutters opening. I rushed to the window and looked out. The moon was bright, and the sky was littered with stars. I could see other parts of the building, as it seemed to be shaped like a horseshoe around an enormous manicured garden. The building itself was made of stone, and there was a tower at the far end that looked like part of a castle. *Was I in a castle?*

I stepped back from the window and looked around the room. To say it was luxurious would be an understatement. I wandered through a door to my left and saw the bathroom, which was enormous. The tub looked like it could hold four people. A second door led to an empty closet, which was nearly the size of my apartment.

I went back into the bedroom, just as Maria was entering. A younger woman followed her, carrying a tray which she set down on the table near the windows.

"Good evening," Maria said cheerfully. "I hope the room is to your liking."

I eyed them warily. "Sure."

"This is Helen." Maria motioned to the other woman, who smiled shyly at me. "She'll be your personal maid. She'll assist you with your clothes, meals, and whatever else you might need."

I didn't understand why I was getting a personal maid. Or why I'd been given such a grand bedroom. Julian was a monster, and I was his prisoner. But I didn't say any of that. Instead I just said, "Hey."

Helen bobbed her head. "Hello miss."

I looked at the tray, which held a wine decanter and a crystal glass. But I knew it wasn't wine.

"I'm sure you're hungry." Maria nodded to Helen, who filled the glass and offered it to me. I took it and forced myself to drink slowly.

Maria watched me with a thoughtful expression. "Julian is busy, but he instructed me to show you around. Or you can explore on your own, if you prefer. It's quite safe. No one here will harm you."

I tried to hide the hope her words gave me. "Um, I'll explore on my own, thanks." *This would be my chance to escape!*

T here was no way I was escaping.

There were guards everywhere outside. They didn't try to stop me, they only nodded respectfully as I walked by. But I knew I couldn't escape without them seeing me. Giving up, I headed back inside.

I wandered through the house, which as it turned out *was* an actual castle. A sprawling medieval structure on the outside, but elegant, modern luxury on the inside. I walked through countless rooms, encountering several servants along the way. They were all in uniform, looking like the maids and footmen from historical movies. Except they were vampires, of course. Some smiled in greeting, but most just bowed their heads. Which was very weird. *Why was everyone bowing?*

I passed through several living rooms. Most of them were formally decorated, but one looked more modern, with a large sectional sofa and a massive tv on the wall. I found an office, which I assumed was Julian's, a library with floor to ceiling shelves containing more books than I could possibly count, and a music room, with a piano and a harp. I ran my fingers softly over the harp strings, longing for my violin, before continuing on.

I discovered a long hall of paintings that looked old and priceless, and an actual ballroom, complete with crystal chandeliers. I finally headed back to my room to find piles of boxes scattered all over the place. Some were big, like the kind of boxes you'd store a wedding dress in. I heard a noise coming from the closet so I popped my head in and saw Helen, hanging up clothes.

"Oh hello, Miss," she said, smiling cheerfully.

"What is this?" I asked, stepping fully into the closet. The shelves that were empty last night were now nearly full.

"Your new wardrobe."

I frowned. "Where did it come from?"

"Mostly Prada and Dior, I think, but-"

"No." I held up a hand to stop her. "I meant, who bought all this?"

Helen blinked. "Julian."

"Why?" I narrowed my eyes at her and she looked down, nervously running her hands down the front of her uniform. I paused. Was *she* scared of *me*? "Nevermind. Thank you for your help."

She smiled, looking relieved. "It's my job, Miss." She turned back to the pile of clothes in front of her.

I went back out into the bedroom, making my way through the scattered boxes. I saw labels that read Chanel, Dior, Prada, and Versace. On the bed were several pink boxes tied with black ribbon. I slid the ribbon off one and lifted the lid to see a pile of black lace, nestled in pink tissue paper. It was a bra and panty set, with a matching garter belt.

"I hope it's to your liking," Julian drawled from behind me.

I yelped and dropped the bra, spinning to face him. He was standing just inside the doorway, with his hands in his pants pockets. He was wearing a black suit again, with a white shirt this time with the top three buttons undone.

We stared at each other. "Why did you buy all this?" I finally asked.

He glanced down at the boxes as he strolled further into the room. "You need clothes. Unless you plan on wearing that every day?" He glanced at me, as I was still in my same clothes from the night before. *Point taken.*

"But why so much? And why so *expensive*?"

He sat down in one of the chairs in front of the window and leaned back casually. "Nothing is expensive to me. I could dress you in diamonds if I wanted to. Which reminds me..."

I clenched my fists at my sides. "You're wrong, if you think this is going to win me over. I still hate you. I'll hate you forever."

He sighed and rubbed a hand over his face. "Forever is a long time. Believe me, I know." He looked at me. "I am not your enemy. I know you *think* I am, but I'm not. *I* did not make you a vampire. I did not capture you and make you stand trial. All *I* did was volunteer to take you. If I hadn't, you would have been executed. Which, might I remind you, is what Adam wanted. When they told him you could be saved through metapherus archond, he asked that you be killed instead."

Julian tilted his head as he looked at me. "Is that what you'd have wanted? Would death be preferable to this?" He gestured to the boxes on the floor.

"Death would be better than being owned by *you*," I snapped. *But would it really?* I put my hands on my hips. "So what now? Now that you *own* me, what do you intend to do with me?"

"Nothing."

I blinked. I hadn't been expecting that.

"In the eyes of the vampire community, you are my property," Julian said. "Which means you will reside here with me. It also means you are under my protection, which is no small thing. No one can touch you now."

I snorted. "No one except you."

"Correct." He stood and walked towards me. "I *can*, but I won't." He came to a stop in front of me, and I had to tip my head back to look at him. He did that a lot, like he was trying to intimidate me with his size.

"Not until you ask me to," he said softly.

"I'll *never* ask you to!" I said angrily.

His lips slowly curved. "We'll see."

CHAPTER 20

The next few nights passed without incident. Julian had disappeared, busy with "business matters," according to Maria. Another load of boxes arrived. It was shoes this time, everything from Nikes to Jimmy Choos. Twenty-two pairs in all.

I continued to explore and eventually got up the courage to question the servants. They all adored Julian, much to my annoyance, and absolutely refused to talk about Valentina. Whenever I asked about her, they clammed right up. One night I was in the music room, missing my violin, when Maria walked in. She knew I'd been questioning the servants about Valentina and wasn't pleased.

"I warn you, not to bring up the subject again," she said, her tone firm.

"I feel like I have the right to know," I told her. "Since Julian said what was done to her will be done to me."

Maria's eyes widened, and she put a hand to her throat. "You must be mistaken. Julian would never-"

"He said it right in front of me."

She seemed flustered by this news. "No one here will talk about Valentina. If you want to know, you'll have to ask Julian."

"And when am I supposed to do that?" I threw up my hands. "He's never here!"

"He'll be back tomorrow night. That's what I came to tell you. We're hosting a ball."

I frowned. "A *ball*."

"Yes."

"An *actual* ball."

"Balls are very common in our world," Maria said. "Vampires are creatures of habit, and since most of us are centuries old..." She shrugged.

Okay then. I was going to a vampire ball.

I stood in my closet the following night, staring at my reflection in the full-length mirror. I could hardly believe it was me looking back.

My gown was emerald green, which made my eyes pop. It was off the shoulder, with a sweetheart neckline that came to a low V in the front, exposing more of my chest that I was comfortable with. It was form fitted to the waist, with long flowing skirts made of silk so fine that they swirled and floated around me when I walked.

Helen had styled my hair into an intricate updo. I feared if I turned my head too fast it would come tumbling down, but she assured me it would stay put the entire evening. On my feet were gold Jimmy Choo stilettos, covered with sparkling crystals.

I twirled slowly from side to side, mesmerized by the way my dress moved. For a moment I felt like Cinderella. Then I remembered it would be Julian escorting me, not a handsome prince. *Not Adam.* I stopped twirling. *Adam was dead, and here I was playing dress up.* I felt tears well, and I blinked furiously.

The sound of someone clearing their throat snapped me out of my melancholy, and I walked into the bedroom to see Julian standing there, wearing a black tux. He looked gorgeous, but that didn't for a second make me forget who he really was.

His eyes traveled over me. "You're breathtaking."

I snorted. "I don't understand why I even have to go to this thing."

He nodded once. "I know, I apologize."

Why was he agreeing with me? It was so much easier to stay mad at him when he showed his true horrible self.

"This ball was planned long before you came into the picture," he explained. "Everyone is curious about you, and our situation. If I canceled now, it would raise suspicion."

"About what?" I asked, genuinely confused.

"About you. Everyone would assume I was hiding you away for some reason. Or that I'd killed you."

My eyes widened. "Why would they assume that?"

He shrugged. "Vampires are suspicious creatures, and they *love* to gossip. The best thing we can do tonight is present ourselves as an amicable couple."

I narrowed my eyes. "But we're not a couple."

"No."

He stepped closer, and I noticed that thanks to my five-inch heels he was only a couple inches taller than me now. *Ha! No more intimidating me with your height!* I decided at that moment to wear heels from then on.

He lifted his hand and ran his fingertips over my collarbone, then lower, brushing the swell of my chest. I leaned away from his touch, but he didn't say anything. Instead, he pulled a sparkling necklace from his pants pocket and fastened around my neck. It felt heavy, and I raised a hand to touch it.

He stepped back and offered me his arm. "Shall we?"

I reluctantly took his arm and let him lead me from the room. The moment we stepped into the hall I could hear the sounds of the party stirring below.

"Tonight will probably be overwhelming for you." He spoke quietly as we walked. "But you have absolutely nothing to fear. We'll mingle and dance, just like at a human party."

I hadn't been to many human parties, but I knew this would be nothing like them.

When we reached the top of the stairs, I saw a crowd of vampires standing around at the bottom. They all turned as one to watch us come down. I gripped Julian's arm tightly, deciding he was the lesser of two evils tonight. *Better the vampire you know, right?*

The ballroom was like a scene from a movie. A string quartet was set up at the far end, and an entire wall of French doors stood open, allowing the night breeze in. It carried the scent of roses with it, and I inhaled deeply.

There were hundreds of vampires present. The men all wore tuxes, but the women were dressed in a variety of styles. Some wore sleek modern dresses, others wore full ball gowns. I couldn't help but stare at the jewels the women were wearing, and I raised a hand to touch my necklace, wishing I'd gotten a better look at it before Julian put it on me.

The other vampires treated Julian like royalty, stepping aside and bowing as he passed. Some women actually curtsied. I gripped his arm, trying to appear calm, even though my heart was pounding. The people were beautiful, but that didn't make me forget they weren't actually *people*.

A waiter passed by and Julian snagged two glasses off his tray, handing me one. Of course it was blood. I wondered where it all came from, enough blood to serve a crowd this size. I took the glass, trying not to think about it. I didn't want to drink here, in front of everyone, and was grateful I'd had a glass in my bedroom before getting dressed.

We stopped several times so Julian could talk to people. Everyone looked at me with curiosity, so I kept my eyes on my wine glass. Everyone wanted a chance to speak with Julian. They hung on his every word like a bunch of groupies.

I stood at his side for what felt like hours, watching the dancers while he talked. Watching vampires dance was hypnotic. They moved with inhuman grace, seeming to float on the air as they spun around the room. It made me wonder how

Adam and I had appeared to the humans in the club the night we went dancing.

The thought of Adam brought me back to reality like a slap to the face. Adam had been executed less than a week ago and here I was at a ball. My chest began to feel tight, and my breathing quickened.

Julian glanced at me. "Excuse me gentlemen," he said, still looking at me. "I think my companion would like to dance." He took me by the hand, and the three vampires he'd been talking to bowed their heads as we walked away. Julian led me to the floor, and the other dancers fell back, leaving a large space cleared for us in the center of the room.

"I don't know how to dance this way," I whispered.

The corner of his mouth curled up as he took me in his arms. "It's easier than it looks."

He swung me in a circle, causing my dress to swish around us. I gasped and gripped him tighter. He moved us around the room, and I was astounded at how easily it came to me. *Did becoming a vampire somehow come with the ability to waltz?*

"Are you alright?" he asked, looking down at my face. "You seemed upset before."

I wasn't about to discuss Adam with him, so I lied. "It's a lot to take in. Remember, two weeks ago I was human, living in my crappy little apartment."

He nodded. "This must be difficult for you. I'm sorry, I should have been more sensitive." I stared at him, surprised by his kindness. "So much time has passed since I was changed, I've all but forgotten what it was like."

Then I was swept away once more. We were in a sea of silk, dresses in every color swirling around us. Jewels sparkled under the chandeliers. And despite myself, I began to have fun. Julian spun me faster and faster, smiling at me in such a devilish way that I actually laughed.

He pulled me closer. "I love the sound of your laugh."

"Oh, really?" I arched an eyebrow at him.

"Really." His tone changed, and I feared we were heading into dangerous territory, so I attempted to change the subject.

"Where have you been all week? It's like you've been avoiding me."

"I have been."

I frowned. "You've been avoiding me? Why?"

He looked down into my eyes as he spoke. "Because I want you, and I know you don't feel the same." My eyes widened, and I quickly glanced away. "When I'm with you, I feel-" he paused. "*Feral*. Like I might lose control."

Oh. Damn.

His eyes fell to my mouth. "It seemed like a good idea to stay away."

My heart was pounding, and I told myself it was from fear. *Liar.* I laughed nervously. "You find me so desirable you had to stay away? I doubt that." Why did I say that? *Was I trying to provoke him? Shut up Sarah!*

"I told you, I never lie."

When the song ended Julian led me off the floor. We were heading towards the exit, and I feared he was taking me somewhere to act on his desires. Just as we made it to the doorway, Maria stepped out of the crowd.

"That dress is amazing," she said, smiling at me.

Julian stopped walking. "Maria, please escort Sarah to her room."

Her smile froze, and her eyes moved back and forth between us. "Of course."

Julian looked at me for a moment, then turned and walked away.

"*Well,*" Maria huffed. "Come on." I followed her out of the room, totally confused. "Did you have a good time?" She asked, looking over her shoulder at me.

I caught up to her, so we were walking side by side. "Yeah, I guess." I glanced at her. "You look incredible, by the way."

She was wearing a black sparkly dress that hugged her body, revealing curves I'd never noticed before, and her hair was loose, hanging in dark waves halfway down her back. Her eyes were heavily lined, and her lips were painted red. She looked ten years younger, and sexy as hell.

She laughed softly. "Thanks."

We walked the rest of the way in silence. She left me at my door and headed back downstairs. I locked my door after she left, even though I knew it wouldn't stop any of the vampires that were downstairs from entering if they wanted to. I just had to hope that Julian was telling the truth when he said no one would harm me.

I undressed, washed my face, and took my hair down. Helen had been right, it had remained beautifully in place the entire evening. I put on some pajama shorts and a camisole top before climbing into bed. I lay there a while, staring up at the ceiling, before getting back up. I was way too wound up to sleep. I sat in one of the chairs in front of the windows and stared out into the night.

I replayed the evening in my mind, feeling confused. Being surrounded by that many vampires had been frightening, but they treated me respectfully. I wondered how they would treat me if Julian wasn't at my side.

The dancing had been dreamlike, and wonderful. I'd actually enjoyed myself. Then Julian told me he wanted me. *And that was bad. Wasn't it?* I pressed my hands to my face, hating the direction my thoughts were heading in. *How could his words excite me?* I flung myself out of my chair and started pacing.

I loved Adam. It had to be some kind of vampire thing that had me wanting Julian all the sudden. I stopped pacing as it dawned on me. *I drank Julian's blood. That's what was causing these feelings. Or maybe he was using his mind control powers to make me feel this way. Was that even possible? Until now, he'd only used his power to call me to him. That's all he said he could do. But what if he lied?* I shook my head. *He never lies. Okay, what if he left that part out?*

I flung myself onto the bed and buried my face in my pillow. I pictured Adam's face and remembered sitting on the porch steps with him at night. I thought about the night at the pond, and when we went dancing.

I rolled onto my back and looked up at the ceiling. *I fell in love with Adam after just five nights, but it was real, wasn't it? Or did I have those feelings because Adam was the one who changed me? Was he the one?* I didn't want to believe it, but after what happened in his cell I could no longer deny it. *Adam made me a vampire. He attacked me in my apartment, and left me to deal with the change alone. I killed a man because of him. I was now the property of another vampire, because of him. I'd never see Allie again, because of him.*

I punched the mattress with my fists and jumped up from the bed. I grabbed my pillow and ripped it half, sending feathers flying everywhere. But it wasn't enough. Rage was boiling up inside of me, and I had to let it out. With a scream, I grabbed a chair and smashed it against the wall, breaking it to pieces. *God, that felt good.* I grabbed the other chair and smashed it, then I picked up the table and threw it across the room. It hit the wall, cracking the plaster.

I continued to demolish my room, destroying everything in sight. I shredded the green dress, littering the floor with torn silk. Then I picked up the loveseat and threw it out the damn window. I heard shouts from below and looked out to see several guards looking up at me. Two disappeared, and I assumed they were going to tell Julian. *Good. I was ready for a fight.* I leaned back against the wall and waited, but he never came.

Eventually my rage wore off, and all that was left was exhaustion. I made my way over to the bed, stepping carefully over pieces of broken furniture. I lay down on the bare mattress, having shredded all the bedding, and curled myself into a ball.

A moment later the steel shutters closed over the windows, and I closed my eyes and soon fell asleep.

CHAPTER 21

I woke sometime later to the sound of Julian's voice. I opened my eyes, but he wasn't there. I sat up on the bed and pushed my hair out of my eyes. I glanced at the windows and saw that the steel shutters were still in place. *It was daytime. I could have sworn-*

Come Sarah.

I stiffened at the sound of his voice in my head. *Damn him!* My body slid off the bed and walked towards the door.

I tried to stop. I almost screamed, but didn't want to draw the attention of any other vampires. As I headed downstairs, I was acutely aware that I was barefoot in my pajamas.

Come to me. I heard his voice again and felt myself being pulled towards him. *Why was he doing this? Was he angry because I trashed my room? Of course those guards told on me!*

I walked further through the house. The lights were all off, and with the shutters closed it was pitch black. But I could see clearly. I was in a long hallway, with a closed door at the end. I knew he was there, waiting.

Come.

I neared a door, and my hand lifted to the knob. My heart was pounding so hard, he could probably hear it through the door. As if in slow motion, my hand turned the knob and pushed the door open, and nothing could have prepared me for what I saw.

The room was draped in jewel colored silk, swaths of it hanging from the ceiling and walls. Small couches were scattered around the room, and the floor was covered with large cushions. The room was full of vampires, all naked, caught up in the throes of passion. In the center of it all stood Julian. He was naked, with a gorgeous woman bent over a chair in front of him. My eyes widened, and I took a step backwards.

Stay.

His lips never moved, but I heard his command clearly. I was frozen to the spot, unable to tear my eyes from his. His eyes were completely black, and his fangs were visible through his parted lips. He held my gaze as he continued to fuck the woman. The sound of her moans filled my ears, and my nipples hardened. Unable to look away, I watched his body move behind hers, his muscles flexing with every thrust. My breathing quickened, and I felt heat curl low in my stomach.

I squeezed my thighs together, and without thinking spoke aloud. "Let me go."

At the sound of my voice, every head in the room jerked towards me. *Shit. That was a mistake.*

My eyes flew back to Julian's. He moved faster, his fingers digging into the woman's hips as he pounded into her. I was breathing harder, practically gasping, as if I were the one getting fucked. I began to wish I was. I wanted to tear Julian off that woman. I wanted to take her place.

Julian's body tensed, and I heard him say my name. *Aloud,* not in my head. Then he released me. I turned and ran from the room. I ran all the way back to my bedroom and slammed the door shut behind me.

What the fuck just happened! I leaned back against the door, listening to see if Julian had followed me. A few minutes passed, but he never came. I told myself it wasn't disappointment I felt. I eventually went to bed, and though I'd never in my life wanted to masturbate so badly, I refused to.

When I finally fell asleep, I dreamed I was back in that crowded room, and Julian had *me* bent over the chair. He fucked me until I came, and suddenly the other vampires disappeared and it was just the two of us. We were laying on the floor, and he was on top of me. We made love slowly, never breaking eye contact.

M y eyes shot open, and I flew upright in bed. I was breathing hard and my chest was heaving. How could I have a dream like that about Julian? I took a deep shuddering breath and tried to calm down. It was a dream. It didn't mean anything. But I couldn't get the tender image out of my mind.

I got up and showered and dressed. By the time I was done, the shutters had opened for the night. There was a soft knock at my door, and Helen walked in carrying a tray for me. She stopped, her mouth dropping open as she saw the destroyed room.

"Uh, yeah, sorry about all this," I said. "Don't worry, I'll clean it up."

She just stood there, continuing to stare at the room, so I walked over and took the tray from her. "Thanks for breakfast, I'll take it from here."

She gave me a bewildered look, then left, closing the door behind her. I sat the tray on the floor and picked up the glass of blood. I sat on the edge of the bed while I drank, waiting to see who'd arrive next. Helen was going to tell *someone.* Plus the guards had seen me through the couch out the window. I'd expected Julian to come up and scold me right after that, but now I knew why he didn't. He'd been busy with *other* things.

I finished drinking and sat there holding the empty glass. A short while later the door swung open and Julian walked in. He stopped, taking in the destruction, then looked at me.

He blew out a breath. "I'm sorry," he said, rubbing a hand over his jaw.

I blinked.

"I should never have called you last night," he continued, stepping into the room. "I wasn't in my right mind-"

I snorted. "No kidding."

"I was high, Sarah. I drank nectar. It's a vampire drug, the only drug that affects us. I was out of my mind. I don't know why I called you. I don't know why I even drank it to begin with, but that's no excuse. I was way out of line, and I'm sorry."

I stared at him, stunned that he was actually apologizing.

He looked around the room. "I can see it upset you."

"Actually, this all happened before that."

His head snapped back towards me. "What happened?"

"I lost my temper, but not with you."

His face hardened. "Who upset you?"

"No one!" I rushed to say. "I was just thinking about stuff and got upset."

He seemed to relax a little. "Can I ask what you were thinking about?"

I looked down at the empty glass I still held. I didn't want to tell him I'd been thinking about Adam.

He let out a breath. "Can we start over?" I looked up at him. "Our time together has been-" He paused, as if searching for the right word. "I know I haven't made the best impression, and my behavior last night has only made things worse."

"I *am* pissed about that." I told him.

"You should be. But do you think we could start fresh? We're going to be stuck together for some time, we might as well try to get along."

I didn't want to get along with him; I wanted to escape. But I nodded. "Okay."

He smiled, looking relieved, and sat on the edge of the bed next to me. "You know, you have a calmness and a level of restraint that is very unusual for a newborn. If it weren't for your scent, I'd have guessed you to be centuries old."

His words were so similar to what Adam once told me, that I felt sad again.

"What is it?" he asked, seeing my expression.

"Is Adam dead?" I asked, fearing his answer.

His expression went blank. "Yes."

"Did you kill him?"

His jaw clenched. "No. But I wish I had."

"How can you say that to me!" I cried, jumping up from the bed.

He stood, his face hardening with anger. "You have no idea what kind of monster he was."

I threw my empty glass to the floor. "He wasn't a monster!"

"Do you forget he's the one that changed you? The pain you felt that night was your body dying. He left you to face death alone, and still you defend him?"

"I love him!" I shouted.

Julian's hand shot out and grabbed my chin, his fingers digging into me painfully. He leaned over me, bringing his face close to mine. "If you ever say his name again, I'll cut out your tongue."

He released me with a shove, and I stumbled backwards before catching myself. He glared at me for a moment, before walking out of the room. He didn't close the door behind him, and I stood there, stunned, staring at the doorway.

What just happened? Why was I defending Adam, when just last night I was so angry at him I trashed my room? Did I just say it to taunt Julian? After what he did to me last night, he deserved it! And one minute he's telling me he wants to start over and be friends, then he's threatening to cut my tongue out? What the actual fuck!

I tried pacing, but my room was too cluttered with broken furniture. I clenched my fists in frustration. *Julian was the monster, not Adam. I saw him rip a man's heart out, and yet everyone seems to worship him? They probably treat him that way because they fear him! Well I don't, and I'll prove it if he ever threatens me again!*

I screamed with frustration and kicked a piece of broken chair. It flew across the room and shattered the one remaining window. *Fuck.*

CHAPTER 22

The next night Julian came to my room to apologize again. My room had been cleaned up and was now bare other than the bed, which I refused to sit on with him, so we stood in the middle of the room facing each other.

I crossed my arms and waited for him to speak.

"Adam is a sore subject." Julian looked around the room as he spoke. "It would be best if you didn't mention him around me. And since he's dead now, there's really no point in discussing him further."

I screamed and flew at him as my tears began to fall. "I hate you!" I screamed, as I hit him over and over.

For a moment he stood there, taking my fury. I raked my nails across his face, leaving trails of blood, and he grabbed my wrists and shook me hard.

"Enough!" He shouted.

I screamed in his face. "I hate you!"

He yanked me against him and slammed his mouth against mine. I could taste his blood as he kissed me, and I struggled to break free. Still pressing his mouth to mine, he backed me up until I was pinned against the wall, then he shoved my head to the side and bit my neck.

"Stop!" I gasped, as desire instantly flared. I knew it was a reaction to his bite, the same thing happened when Adam bit me, but I shouldn't be feeling it with Julian. I wanted to keep struggling, but my body relaxed against his. He pressed his hips against me and I moaned, spreading my legs to let him get closer.

He grabbed my ass with both hands, lifting me, and I wrapped my legs around his waist. He pulled his fangs from my neck and kissed my mouth again. This time I kissed him back, tasting my blood, mixed with his. I moaned into his mouth and grabbed him by the hair, holding him close, but he pulled back, breaking the kiss. I leaned forward, trying to reclaim his mouth, but he pulled away again. I whimpered with frustration as he slowly lowered me to the floor.

"What's wrong?" I asked, reaching for him again.

He put his hands on my shoulders, gently holding me back. "You're reacting to my venom. This isn't really what you want."

"It is," I insisted, reaching for him again.

He shook his head regretfully. "It's not."

He left after that, and when I finally regained my senses, I was disgusted with myself. Feeling the need to clear my head, I went outside to walk in the gardens.

The guards paid me no mind as I passed, as though I hadn't nearly smashed them with a flying couch the night before. I wandered into the gardens until I found a private spot with a stone bench, where I sat down with a sigh.

Being a vampire was hard. I had no control over my emotions. I was falling in and out of love in the blink of an eye. Or maybe it was never love. Maybe vampires couldn't love. Maybe they just gave in to the desires that arose when they fed from each other. I wished there was someone I could ask about these things. I felt like a girl, going through puberty without a mother to talk to. Who was going to teach me the birds and the bees, vampire style?

I spent the rest of the night in the garden, feeling sorry for myself.

The following night when Helen arrived with my tray, she informed me I needed to get ready because Julian was taking me on a trip. She packed my bags while I showered and dressed, and a short while later I was heading downstairs to meet Julian. I found him talking to another vampire, who I'd seen around the house a few times. Julian smiled when he saw me, and the other guy walked away.

"Hey," I said, feeling awkward after throwing myself at him the night before. "Where are we going?"

"To an island I own, about an hour from here."

I stared at him. "You *own* an island?"

"Two, actually. One's off the coast of Ireland."

Stunned by his casual admission, I followed him down to the parking garage where we climbed into his limo and headed for the airport. Before long we were in the jet, flying over the ocean. We didn't speak for most of the flight, but I felt his eyes on me as I stared out the window. The sea sparkled in the moonlight, and it wasn't long before I saw an island in the distance. It was much larger than I'd imagined, and as we neared, I could see a long stretch of beach and several buildings.

A jeep was waiting for us when we landed. Julian got behind the wheel and I climbed into the passenger seat.

"Ready?" He flashed me a grin, and I nodded. His good mood was so at odds with what I'd seen so far, it had me flustered and confused.

As we drove off the runway, the road headed into what looked like a tropical jungle. Palm trees swayed overhead, and lush vegetation lined the sides of the road. I looked out into the trees as we drove, keeping my face turned away from him.

After a few minutes, we pulled up in front of a large house made of dark reddish brown wood. A line of servants stood out front, wearing neatly pressed uniforms.

Julian turned off the engine before hopping out and coming around to open my door. "You're going to love it here," he said, taking my hand.

He nodded to the servants as he led me up the stairs into the house. When we entered the building, I stopped in my tracks. It was stunning. The ceilings soared at least 20 feet high, and large leaf shaped ceiling fans lazily stirred the air. The wood floors gleamed, and the entire far wall was a water feature, with water cascading down into a bed of smooth polished stones.

Julian turned to look at me. "Come on, I'll show you around."

I didn't want him to show me around, but I didn't have much choice in the matter. We spent the next couple of hours walking around the property, and I found myself relaxing. Staying angry was difficult when I was surrounded by such beauty. We started in the main house, with the stunning water feature, then Julian showed me several smaller guest villas. Stone pathways cut through the jungle, connecting all the buildings, and at the center of it all was an enormous infinity pool, overlooking the ocean.

"How do you afford all this?" I asked, looking past the pool to the sea beyond. "Do you have a job? Or is this all from *vampire investments*?" Adam had told me that's how most vampires made their money.

Julian laughed and sat down on a lounge chair. "I inherited a rather enormous fortune from my sire, who was killed long ago." I sat on a chair next to him and twisted sideways to face him. He crossed his arms behind his head and leaned back in his chair. "But, yes, I have many investments and businesses that continue to grow my fortune."

I shook my head in disbelief. "It seems like you have enough to retire at this point."

He glanced at me. "I'm the head of a large family, responsible for nearly six hundred vampires." My mouth dropped open, and he chuckled. "Yeah, I know. It's a lot."

A lot? "You changed *six hundred* people into vampires?"

"God no! But I'm the eldest of my siblings, therefore responsible for them and any vampires they create."

"Oh. How many siblings do you have?"

"Ninety-one."

"Damn, that's a lot. I only have one."

He lowered his arms, and his expression turned thoughtful. "Would you like to talk about them?"

I looked away. "No." I stared at the ocean, picturing Allie's face, remembering her laugh, and suddenly realized I *did* want to talk about her. Badly.

"My sister's name is Allie," I said, without looking at him. "She's two years younger than me, and…. perfect." I laughed, sadly. "I don't mean that in a snarky way. She really is perfect. She's the warmest, kindest, person I've ever known. She always puts others before herself, and she's *so* optimistic, no matter how bad things get. She's funny, and beautiful-" I stopped, blinking at the tears in my eyes. "And now she's all alone."

"What about your parents?" he asked softly.

I just shook my head, unable to speak past the lump in my throat. We sat quietly for a while, while I regained control of my emotions.

"How old are you?" I asked after a while.

"I am one thousand and ninety years old."

I shot upright on my chair. "*Are you serious?*"

He laughed. "Yeah, I'm old."

"Damn!" I leaned back in my chair again. "I can't even wrap my mind around that." I turned on my side to face him. "What's it like? I mean, how does it feel? You've lived through so much of history. You've seen the world change. It must have been amazing." Then I frowned, thinking of all the wars that took place over the last thousand years. "And scary. And sad."

He stared at me. "I couldn't have described it better myself. It *has* been amazing, and scary, and sad."

The way he said it made me want to reach out and touch his hand. To comfort him somehow. Instead, I changed the subject. "So I guess you can fly, then?"

The corner of his mouth curled up. "Yes. I can daywalk too."

"You can go out in the sun?" Adam told me only the oldest, most powerful vampires could do that.

"I can."

"How old do I have to get before I can daywalk?" Adam was over two hundred years old and he still couldn't.

Julian shrugged. "It's different for everyone. It's not just about age, it also depends on how powerful the vampire who changed you was. My sire was changed by one of the original eight, so it happened sooner for me than most."

"What's the original eight?"

"The first eight vampires, changed by our king."

My eyes widened. "You have a *king*? Um, I'm going to need a lot more information about that."

Julian chuckled. "Our king is the original vampire. No one knows how he was created, or even *if* he was created. Maybe he was never human. Maybe he's a god." He shrugged. "He is the most powerful of us all, by far. He has power over *everyone,* vampire and human alike. He can control our bodies, and hear our thoughts. He can turn a vampire to dust, just by looking at them."

I shuddered. "I hope I never have to meet him."

"You don't need to worry about that. He never leaves his estate. It's been hundreds of years since anyone's seen him."

Thank god for that! "So the original eight, do I have to worry about them?"

"You already met three, at your trial."

I looked at him, confused, before it dawned on me. "The Strategoi."

He nodded. "The original eight became the Strategoi. Since they were turned by our king, they are the most powerful in the world. Two have since died, and their positions were given to the next in line."

I frowned as I thought. "So you were created by a vampire, who was created by one of the original eight, which means the vampire king is your... great-grandfather?"

He laughed. "Yeah, I guess. I certainly wouldn't address him as such."

"Is that why everyone bows to you, and acts like you're something special?"

He arched an eyebrow. "You don't think I'm special?"

I rolled my eyes.

"Yes," he said. "They show respect because I'm next in line should one of the Strategoi die."

Damn.

We talked all night, out by the pool. I wanted to know absolutely everything about the world of vampires, and he answered every question I had. When it was time for bed, he walked me to my room and left me at the door. As I lay in bed, waiting to fall asleep, I couldn't stop thinking about the fact that the ninth most powerful vampire in the world was sleeping down the hall from me. I wanted to hang on to my hatred for him, but It had been such a pleasant night, I was starting to think we actually *could* be friends.

CHAPTER 23

I dreamed of Julian that night. Of his dark eyes and his sexy mouth. I was lying on the bed and he was kneeling over me. His fingers were inside of me, teasing me, and I arched my hips off the bed, crying his name as I came apart.

A loud bang woke me, and I shot up in bed. My bedroom door was still shaking from being flung against the wall, and Julian stood in the doorway, his fangs descended. I shrieked and scuttled back against the headboard.

His eyes swept the room before landing on me.

"You screamed." He stepped into the room and started walking towards the bed. His fingers were curled, and I saw claws at their tips.

"No." I shook my head quickly.

He stopped walking and inhaled deeply. His lips parted. *He knew.*

"You screamed my name," he said softly, coming to stand at the edge of the bed.

"I had a nightmare," I lied. "I was scared."

He inhaled again, and a wicked smile spread across his face. "You don't smell scared."

I squeezed my thighs together, and his eyes fell to my lap. He grabbed the edge of the sheet and slowly pulled it off of me. He stood there, looking down at my body, and his chest began to rise and fall more rapidly. I felt my own breath quicken in response, and I shifted on the bed, fighting the urge to spread my legs for him.

His hands fisted at his sides. "Tell me to stay," he said, his voice rough.

My heart was pounding. I *wanted* him to stay. "Leave."

For a moment I thought he'd refuse. He stared at me, the muscle in his jaw ticking. Then he turned to go.

"*Stay.*" My voice was barely a whisper, but he heard it. His body tensed and he slowly turned back around. I knew then I was in trouble.

In one smooth motion, he grabbed my hips and pulled me away from the headboard so that I was laying across the bed. He climbed up over me, bracing his hands on either side of my head, and lowered his mouth to mine. He parted my lips with his tongue, and I wrapped my arms around his neck and pulled him down against me, needing to feel his body. I arched against him, and he cupped my breast with his hand, rubbing his thumb over my hardened nipple.

He broke our kiss and sat back long enough to pull my camisole over my head, then he lowered his mouth to my breast. He took my nipple in his mouth, swirling his tongue around it, and I moaned, grabbing his head to hold him close. He pulled back, and I whimpered in protest, but he was only moving to my other breast. He nipped at my nipple with his teeth and I cried out. I felt dizzy with lust.

"I want you now," I panted, reaching for his shorts.

"Mmmm," he growled against my nipple. "So impatient." He sat up once more to pull my underwear off, and I took advantage of his upright position to yank his shorts down. My eyes widened at the sight of his erection, then flew to his. His lips slowly curved. He knew what he was packing.

He tossed my underwear over his shoulder and leaned back down, pushing me back against the mattress once more. He kissed me again and began to move against me, sliding his length against my wetness. And *god* I was wet. I bent my knees, lifting them, wanting him inside of me. I could feel his lips move against mine, and I knew he was smiling.

"Not yet," he murmured against my mouth. He kissed his way down my neck, and I turned my head to the side, hoping he would bite me. He growled again. "So tempting." He moved lower, teasing my nipples for a moment before continuing down my body.

Fuck yes. I closed my eyes, ready for what I knew was coming. He kissed his way down my stomach, stopping to lick my navel.

"Julian," I breathed, wanting more.

"I love hearing my name on your lips," he whispered against my skin. "I want you to say it when I make you come." He lowered his head further and wrapped his powerful hands around my thighs. He inhaled deeply and when he exhaled I could feel his breath on my clit. Then I felt his tongue.

I moaned loudly at his first touch. I was so aroused I felt like I was already about to come. He ran his tongue down my center, then back up, circling my clit.

"Fuck," I breathed, fisting my hands in his hair, holding him where I wanted him.

He dipped lower and pushed his tongue inside of me, groaning as he did, and I gasped and arched off the bed. He gripped my thighs tighter, holding me in place, and swirled his tongue around my clit. Small circles that drove me insane.

"Don't stop!" I gasped. I was breathing so hard I could barely speak. He lifted his head, and I cried out in protest.

"I want to be inside of you when I make you come for the first time." He moved up, positioning himself, and looked into my eyes as he slowly slid into me.

"Fuuuuck." I moaned, feeling him stretch me.

His lips curved. He knew what he was doing to me. He moved slowly, sliding almost all the way out before pushing back in, making me gasp with every thrust. It was a lot to take, but I wanted more.

"Faster," I breathed, digging my finger into his hips. "Faster."

He obeyed, quickening his pace until I could take no more.

I cried his name when I came, my body tightening around his cock. I felt his teeth pierce my neck, and I cried out again. Stars exploded behind my eyelids as my senses spun out of control. I could hear my blood rushing through his veins. Everywhere our bodies touched, my nerve endings were vibrating with pleasure, and my pussy continued to clench around him from an orgasm that seemed to have no end. Just when I thought I could take no more he stiffened and moaned against my neck.

He retracted his fangs and licked the wounds on my neck. I lay beneath him, panting, feeling dazed. He kissed my mouth and I could taste my blood. Slowly he slid out of me, his movement making me quiver again. I looked up at him, not knowing what to say. What was there I possibly *could* say?

He looked at me with an intensity that took my breath away. "You belong to me," he whispered harshly.

"Yes." In that moment I did belong to him. And he belonged to me.

CHAPTER 24

When I woke up, he was gone. I stared at the ceiling wondering how I would face him again. *How could I be so stupid? In less than a day, I went from hating Julian to fucking him! And so soon after Adam? Was I really moving on that fast? Then again, what was there to move on from? I'd only known Adam a few days, and he'd lied to me the entire time. It was his fault I was in this mess!*

I threw off the blankets and got out of bed, but my troubled thoughts followed me as I went into the bathroom to take a shower. Afterwards, I put on some shorts and a tank top, and went in search of Julian.

I found him in the kitchen, placing a bottle of blood and two glasses on a serving tray. He was barefoot, wearing loose black shorts and no shirt, and my mouth watered at the sight of him.

He smiled when he saw me. "I was just coming back."

I tore my eyes away from his bare chest and continued into the room. "About what happened," I began, looking anywhere but at him. "It didn't mean anything, right? It was just sex." I glanced at him, but his face had gone blank. "I mean, I was all worked up from my dream. I think we both know it wasn't a nightmare." I looked at him expectantly, but he remained silent. "It's just that I just met you and we don't really know each other, and everything is changing so fast, and I don't know what I'm feeling, and I'm super confused about you, and about Adam, and why aren't you saying anything?"

"I think you've said it all," he said quietly. He poured blood into the two glasses before walking over and handing one to me. I took it, and he continued past me out of the room.

I stood there like an idiot, not knowing if I should follow. *Was he angry? Did I hurt his feelings?* I shook my head and downed the blood, feeling more confused than ever, then I put my glass down and went after him. I searched all over the house, and out by the pool before finally asking one of the servants where he was. They told me he was probably at the beach, so that's where I went.

I walked down onto the beach, but he wasn't there. I saw something dark in the sand and walked over to it. As soon as I picked it up, I realized it was Julian's shorts. My eyes darted around and there he was, coming up from below the surface, about thirty feet offshore.

He saw me right away and lifted his hands to push his wet hair back from his face as he walked towards the shore. The water became more shallow as he approached, exposing more and more of him, until it became apparent that he wasn't wearing a swimsuit. *Because I was holding his shorts.* I looked away as he approached, staring off into the distance until I felt him tug his shorts out of my hand.

"Sarah."

I shot him a quick glance and saw that he'd put his shorts on. "I want to talk." I blurted, before he could say anything.

"Me too."

I blinked. "You do?"

He nodded. "I answered all of your questions last night. Now it's your turn to answer some of mine."

I'd intended to talk about what happened between us, but okay. "Fire away," I said, sitting down in the sand.

He sat down next to me and leaned back on his elbows, stretching his long legs out in front of him. "I want to know about your life, before you were changed. I want to know about your family, and Allie."

So I told him. I skimmed over the sad parts about my parents, choosing instead to regale him with funny stories about Allie and I as kids. I told him about my violin, and how much my music had meant to me. How sometimes when I played, I felt like my mother was with me.

I grew quiet after that, and he moved closer and wrapped an arm around me. I let him hold me, grateful for the comfort he provided. We stayed that way for hours, silently watching the ocean. Just before dawn we walked back to the house. We didn't speak or touch on the way back, but it felt nice just being next to him.

He walked me to my bedroom door and said goodnight. Just as he was turning to leave I said, "Tell me about Valentina." He stiffened, but didn't turn back around.

"Who was she?" I asked. "What happened to her?"

"She's not your concern," he said, his back still to me. "Do not ask again."

I watched him walk away, and wanted to scream with frustration. I'd just poured my heart out to him on the beach and he wouldn't answer one stupid question! I went into my room and slammed my door behind me. I slammed it so hard the frame cracked and the door bounced back open and flew backwards into the wall.

"Shit," I mumbled, seeing the hole the doorknob left in the wall. I went over and tried to close the door, but it wouldn't latch due to the broken frame. "Shit."

When I woke the next night, I didn't know what to expect. Was Julian going to be in a good mood when I saw him, or was he still pissed? Life with him was an emotional roller-coaster.

I showered and dressed, choosing a white camisole and a flowy blue skirt that hit just below my knees. Deciding to forego shoes, I went in search of Julian.

I found him in the living room, sitting on a dark leather couch, with a bunch of papers spread out on the coffee table in front of him. He was reading something, but he dropped the paper when I entered the room.

"I-"

"I'm sorry," he said, interrupting me. I paused, not sure what to say. He ran a hand over his jaw. "I feel like I'm always apologizing to you. You have every right to ask about Valentina. Please sit down."

I perched on the edge of a leather armchair. *Was he finally going to tell me about her?* I was positively buzzing with anticipation.

"Valentina was changed by her sister, who was one of the original eight. When I met her she'd been a vampire for one hundred and sixty years. We fell in love, and she changed me. For the longest time it was just the two of us, and we were happy. There weren't many of us back then, a couple hundred maybe. As more vampires were created, a hierarchy fell into place, and not everyone was happy about it. A few vampires started changing humans like crazy, creating families so large and powerful that no one could control them. They were creating armies. Feeling threatened, Valentina decided to do the same. But it changed her."

He tipped his head back and looked up at the ceiling. "The world was a cruel place back then. She lost a little of her humanity with every vampire she created. But I still loved her." He looked at me. "Until Adam killed her."

I stared at him. It couldn't be true. Adam would never kill someone. "Why?" I whispered.

"Because he blamed her for his fiance's death."

"I don't understand." My heart was thundering. *Adam was engaged?*

"Valentina changed Adam, but he did not transition well. He killed his fiance, and blamed Valentina for it, since she was the one who made him a vampire."

My mind was buzzing. "I don't believe you. He would have told me."

Julian laughed harshly. "Because he was so honest with you about everything else?"

He had a point.

"He killed Valentina, in such a horrific way-" He closed his eyes, his expression pained.

Seeing him like that did something to me. I stood and walked around the coffee table to sit down beside him. I put my arms around him and laid my head against his chest. After a moment he wrapped his arms around me and rested his head atop mine.

I wasn't about to apologize for what Adam had done. If Valentina hadn't changed him, he wouldn't have killed his fiance. Adam once told me he wasn't given a choice when he was changed, and if that was true, Valentina was one hundred percent to blame. But Julian had loved her, so I offered him comfort.

I could feel Julian's heartbeat against my cheek as I held him, and my own heart began to beat in tune with his.

After a while he lifted his head and I leaned back to look up at him. "I have a gift for you," he said.

I leaned back further, releasing him. *He had a gift for me?*

He slid to the edge of the couch and reached down to lift something off the floor. It was a violin case. My eyes widened when I saw it. He handed it to me and I ran my hand over the case before opening it.

I gasped when I saw the instrument. It was a Palo Greiner violin. An instrument I had only ever dreamed of playing.

"Where did you get this?" I ran my fingertips over the smooth wood, in awe of its beauty.

He looked at me hopefully. "Do you like it?"

"I love it," I breathed. "How did you get this so fast? I only told you I played violin last night."

He smiled. "You can thank Maria for that. She's a miracle worker." I shook my head in disbelief. "Would you play for me?" he asked.

I nodded and carefully took the violin out of its case. My heart began to pound as I stood. I felt suddenly shy, and was confused by it. I'd never been shy or insecure when it came to my music. Why was I feeling that way now?

"Any requests?" I half-joked, trying to shake my nerves.

He just smiled and leaned back against the couch.

I took a few steps away, fidgeting. *God, what was wrong with me?* I felt bare and exposed. I closed my eyes and imagined that I was alone. I drew the bow across the strings, and as soon as I heard those first notes, I was calm. The violin felt like it was made for me. Like it was part of me. The rest of the world faded away, until I was alone in the dark with my music. When the song ended, I opened my eyes and looked at Julian.

His eyes were focused on my face, his expression intense. "Play it again."

I looked at him with confusion. "The same song?"

"Yes."

I played it again. Then I played another song, and another. I played for hours, at Julian's urging, until my internal clock told me that sunrise was approaching.

I stopped mid-song and looked at him with wide eyes. I had played the entire night, and my hands weren't sore or tired.

"You're incredible," he said, standing. "The way you play- I was transported." My heart swelled with pride at his words.

"I mean it Sarah," he continued. "Talented musicians are a dime a dozen in our world. Vampires have centuries to master their craft. But you... Watching you play felt like magic."

I didn't know what to say. His words touched me. I felt so close to him at that moment, I was afraid if I spoke I'd say something I'd regret. I looked away.

"I think it's almost sunrise," I said, as I gently placed the violin in its case and laid it on the coffee table.

"You can take that to your room if you want." He nodded towards the case. "It belongs to you."

Neither of us spoke as he walked me to my room. We were so close as we walked, our bodies nearly touching. Thoughts were flying through my mind a million miles per second. *Naughty thoughts.* Memories of the night before.

When we got to my door, I looked up at him and our eyes met. I wanted so badly to know what he was thinking.

"Well, goodnight," I finally said.

"Can I stay?" he asked.

His words nearly made my legs give out. "Yes."

He lowered his head and brushed his lips softly across mine. I rose on my tiptoes and wrapped one arm around his neck, my other hand still holding the violin. I pressed my lips to his, and he groaned. He grabbed me and lifted me off the floor, and I wrapped my legs around his waist.

Without breaking our kiss, he opened the door with one hand and kicked it closed behind us. It bounced off its cracked frame and swung back open, but neither of us cared.

His tongue swept into my mouth as he carried me towards the bed. He lay me down and straightened to look down at me. I watched his pupils dilate until his eyes were completely black, and I shuddered with anticipation.

He roughly yanked his shirt over his head, and I went to do the same before realizing I still had the handle of the violin case clasped in my fist. I released it and pushed it towards the bottom of the bed before yanking my tank top off.

He leaned over to grab the waistband of my skirt, and I lifted my hips, allowing him to pull it off me. He tossed it to the floor, then he wrapped his hands around my legs and pulled me towards him. I let out a yelp of surprise, and his mouth curled into a wicked grin.

He pulled me snug up against him, my legs spread wide and dangling off the bed on either side of him. He grabbed my underwear with both hands and tore the fabric, ripping them right off me. He looked down to where our bodies meet, and I wriggled my hips, wishing his shorts weren't in the way. He ran his hands up my thighs, then he pushed my legs wide. I started to sit up, to reach for his shorts, but he pushed me back against the mattress.

"Not yet," he said, shaking his head. Then he dropped to his knees.

My eyes closed as he brought his mouth down on me. He moaned against my flesh, and his hands slid under my ass, lifting me off the bed. He pushed his tongue inside me, and my hands fisted in the blankets. He tortured me with his tongue, until I screamed his name, then he turned his head slightly and sank his fangs into me. I grabbed his head, holding him to me as he drank.

The tremors from my orgasm were just beginning to fade when he pushed two fingers deep inside of me. I gasped, my eyes flying open, and tension immediately started to build again as he slid his fingers in and out of me. My body tightened around his fingers, and I knew I was about to come again. He must have known it too, because he withdrew his fangs from my body and flicked his tongue over my clit. I went spiraling over the edge, lifting my hips to thrust against his hand. My body was still throbbing when he removed his fingers and stood to slide his cock into me.

There was no slow teasing this time. He pounded into me with inhuman speed, never giving my body time to recover. He stood at the edge of the bed, gripping my thighs, holding my legs up and spreading them as he wrecked me. I watched him through the red haze of lust, marveling at the site of his body. After two powerful orgasms, and the effect of his venom, I was too weak to do anything but lay there as he sought his release. I watched his face as he came, loving that I was the cause of his pleasure.

CHAPTER 25

The next few nights flew by. We swam naked in the ocean, which of course led to other things. I played violin for him, and he taught me a dice game from the middle ages which quickly turned naughty. I discovered gambling could be fun when the loser had to pay up with sexual favors. I began to suspect he was losing on purpose. Every night we talked for hours, and when dawn approached, I fell asleep in his arms.

One night, while we were lounging by the pool, Julian informed me we'd be returning home the following evening. One of his siblings was getting married and there would be a week-long celebration.

His announcement surprised me. I hadn't realized vampires got married, and when I said as much, he laughed. "It's not as common for us, as it is for humans, but it lasts a lot longer."

I rolled my eyes playfully. "Sure, when you're immortal."

He turned his head to look at me, his expression becoming serious. "Vampires take their vows seriously. Divorce doesn't exist in our world."

I rolled onto my side on my lounge chair, so I was fully facing him. "How do you know you're choosing the right person?

Staying married for a few decades is hard for humans. How do you manage it for centuries? What if you grow apart?"

"We're not human, Sarah. We don't love the same. When two vampires fall in love, something inside of them clicks, like two halves of a whole coming together."

I'd had that exact thought about Adam, that I became whole when I was with him. The reminder tugged at my heart and I rolled onto my back to look up at the sky.

"What is it?" Julian asked.

I just shook my head.

"Sarah." He swung his legs off his chair and sat up, facing me.

I shook my head again. "I'm so confused, and have no one to talk to."

"You can talk to me."

I laughed, harshly. "Can I?" I shot him a look. "About Adam?"

A muscle ticked in his jaw. "Yes."

I sat up and turned sideways on my chair so that I was facing him. "Okay." I paused, not knowing where to begin, or how much I should reveal. "I thought I loved Adam, after only a few nights. When I was human, I would have laughed at that. I'd have said it was impossible to fall that fast. But when I was with him it felt real."

Julian opened his mouth to say something, but I cut him off. "And now I'm with you, and I feel-" I shrugged and looked away.

"How do you feel?" he asked softly.

"I feel... A lot." I threw my hands up in frustration. "How can I feel this way with you, when I felt that way with Adam? And if what I felt with him was only a reaction to his blood, how do I know my feelings for you aren't the same? The second I tasted your blood I wanted you. I wanted you so bad I'd have let you fuck me right there in that cell, with Adam chained to the wall. And what happens if I drink from another vampire? Will I fall in love with him too? How can I tell what's real?"

Julian held up a hand to stop me. "First of all, you will never drink from another vampire. You belong to me, for better or worse."

Part of me wanted to slap him for the reminder, but another part of me was thrilled.

"Maybe you did love him," he said, surprising me. "Vampires fall fast, and hard. It's like our animal side instinctually recognizes our mate when we meet them. But it's also true that our blood is an aphrodisiac to other vampires. That's why we feed during sex. You would've desired Adam as soon as you drank his blood, which happened when he changed you."

I was confused. "What do you mean, I drank his blood when he changed me?"

"When Adam changed you he drank nearly all of your blood. When you were at the verge of death, he would have cut or bit himself and fed you his own blood. That is how we are created. When his blood filled your empty veins, you were changed.

I squeezed my hands into fists and felt my nails cut into my skin. "None of it was real. He orchestrated everything, and I fell for it."

Julian reached over and took my hands in his. "There's no way you could have known. You weren't even aware vampires existed."

I stared at our clasped hands. "Then how can I trust what I feel for you? Is it real? Or is it because I drank your blood?"

"What do you feel for me?" he asked softly.

I wasn't going to admit that it felt like love, so I lied. "I don't know."

He gave my hands a little squeeze. "Then say nothing. Let's just enjoy being together."

I knew it wouldn't be that easy, but I nodded. "Okay."

The next night we flew home. When we arrived back at the castle, Maria was waiting.

"I need to speak with you," she told Julian, the second we walked in the door.

He sighed heavily. "Can it wait?"

She glanced at me, then back at him. "No."

He pressed a kiss to my hair. "You head up. I'll be up shortly."

I nodded and headed for the stairs as Maria followed Julian down the hall towards his office. But I didn't have to wait long. Julian walked into my room only a few minutes after me.

I smiled as he entered, then I saw his expression. "What's wrong?"

"Nothing serious," he said, looking around the room. "But we need to leave again. There's been some trouble, and I need to go handle things."

"And you want me to go with you?"

His head jerked towards me. "Yes."

I blinked, surprised by his tone. "Okay."

He ran a hand over his jaw. "I'm sorry, I shouldn't be snapping at you." He gave me a small smile and stepped towards me, reaching for my hands. "I want you to come with me. When I've handled my business, we can enjoy ourselves. London is wonderful this time of year."

"London!" I smiled excitedly. "I've always wanted to go to London!"

"Good!" He pulled me closer, wrapping his arms around me. "I can't wait to show you around." He dropped a kiss on the tip of my nose. "I'll send Helen up so she can help you get packed."

"Now?" I asked, wanting more than a nose kiss.

"Yep." He swatted my ass before walking out of the room.

Okay. I was going to London.

CHAPTER 26

Maria, Helen, and three male vampires flew with us. I'd seen the guys around the house a few times, but wasn't sure who they were or what exactly they did for Julian.

Julian's London home was the penthouse of a luxury high-rise building. The entire outer wall was glass, giving us an unparalleled view of the city. Maria and the three guys left as soon as we arrived, and Julian gave me a tour while Helen disappeared into the bedroom to unpack our things.

We climbed into bed just before sunrise. I was nervous about the lack of steel shutters over the windows, but Julian assured me that the drapes were one hundred percent blackout. I was still scared though. What if someone came in and opened the blinds when we were sleeping?

He'd laughed at that. "What, like vampire hunters? You've seen too many movies."

Then he found a way to distract me from my fear.

The next night Julian left to take care of his problem. I stayed home, watching Netflix all night. I watched four hours of Schitt's Creek, then just for laughs, I decided to watch Dracula. Only I didn't laugh. I made it halfway through before I shut off the tv and threw the remote on the floor. The violent scenes seemed too real now, and the romance too sad. I thought about putting Schitt's Creek back on to cheer myself up, but decided against it. Instead, I curled up in a chair and stared out the window.

I realized something was wrong when the drapes automatically closed over the windows, blocking my view. It was almost sunrise and Julian wasn't back. I stood up and started pacing. When I heard the door open, I spun around, relieved. But it was only Maria.

She paused when she saw me. "Julian has been detained."

"With what?" I asked. "The sun is almost up!"

"I'm sure he's told you he's a daywalker."

"Yeah."

"Well, there you have it. He'll be fine."

"When will he be back?" I asked.

She slid her feet out of her high heels and bent to pick them up. "I don't know."

"Well, where did he go?"

"I don't know."

"You don't know or you won't tell me?"

She sighed, sounding tired. "I work for Julian, Sarah. I can't discuss his private matters with anyone. Not even you. Goodnight." She walked away, down the hall towards the room she was staying in.

I went into my room, *Julian's* room, and closed the door. I glanced nervously at the closed drapes, before changing into my pajamas and climbing into bed. I thought about slipping between the sheets naked, then decided Julian didn't deserve to come home to that, after making me worry.

W hen I woke up the next evening Julian's side of the bed was still empty. I got up and went out into the living area and saw Helen and Maria in the kitchen. They both stopped talking when I walked in.

"Good morning. I mean-" I shrugged and looked around the kitchen, suddenly wishing I could have a cup of coffee. "Julian already left again? Or did he never come home?"

"He'll return as soon as he's able," Maria said.

"O-kaay." I drew out the word. "So what's the plan for tonight then? Do you guys want to go out? You could show me around?" I looked at them hopefully.

Maria shook her head. "I'm sorry. You're to remain here until Julian returns."

"And when will that be?"

She gave me a look. "I don't know."

I looked at Helen, hoping for support, but she quickly looked away. *What the hell was going on?* "Okay." I said, with a shake of my head. I turned around and went back to the bedroom, where I started to pace.

Where was he? And why couldn't I go out without him? Was he afraid I'd run away? Was that how it was going to be with us? I'd never get to go anywhere without him because I was his property? After our time on the island, I thought things would be different.

The more I paced, the more I thought, the more worked up I got. I was so mad when the bedroom door finally swung open that I bared my fangs. But it was only Helen.

"I'm sorry!" she said, quickly stepping backwards.

I covered my mouth with my hand. "I'm sorry! I thought you were Julian!" I tried to make my fangs retract, but they wouldn't.

"It's okay." She hesitantly stepped into the room. She held out the glass she was carrying. "I thought you might be hungry."

I took the glass with one hand, still covering my mouth with the other. "I'm sorry, I don't know how to make them go away."

She smiled kindly. "You have to relax." She stepped closer, looking more at ease. "Feeding will help." She pointed at the glass I held.

Feeling foolish, I took a drink. When the glass was empty, she held out a hand, and I gave it to her. She was right, I did feel calmer. I felt my fangs retract, and I flopped down on the foot of the bed.

"I'm sorry," I said again. "I don't know why I'm so upset. I don't know what's wrong with me."

She smiled again. "When vampires fall in love, they can become... *possessive* over one another. It's natural for you to be upset when you don't know where he is or what he's doing.

Just like it's natural for *him* to want you to stay here, where it's safe, when he's not around to protect you."

I sighed. "Now I feel foolish." Then her words caught up to me. "And who says we're in love?"

Helen only smiled and walked out of the bedroom.

I spent the entire night in the bedroom, thinking over Helen's words, and worrying about Julian. When dawn approached again and Julian still wasn't back, I was terrified.

What if something happened to him? Something *must* have happened. He wouldn't leave me here this long, without saying anything. I crawled into bed and buried my face in his pillow, inhaling his scent. When I finally fell asleep, I dreamed I was back at my trial, watching Julian rip the guard's heart out.

When I woke the next night I felt troubled by my dream. I didn't bother leaving the bedroom to talk to Maria. I knew I'd get no information from her. I was standing at the window when Helen came in with *breakfast*. I was angry and didn't want to take it out on her, so I never turned around. She quietly set the glass down and left. I spent the entire night in my room.

When I woke on the fourth night, I knew I wasn't alone. I opened my eyes and saw him sitting in a chair by the window, watching me. I sat up and pushed my hair out of my face. I'd been so angry, but seeing him now all I felt was relief that he was safe.

I looked him over, noticing his dirty clothes and rumpled appearance. "What happened?"

"I'm fine."

Well, so much for relief, now I was pissed. "You're not going to tell me anything?" I let him know by my tone how I felt about that.

His eyes narrowed, ever so slightly. "My business doesn't concern you."

"Business. *Right.*" I flung the blankets off me and got out of bed on the opposite side, away from him. I put my hands on my hips as I faced him. "Business that kept you away for three nights and made it impossible for you to call? Business so secretive that apparently Maria isn't allowed to tell me about it? And why the hell couldn't I go out without you?" I was nearly shouting by that point.

Julian pushed himself out of his chair. "I don't have to explain myself to you."

"Of course not," I sneered. "I'm just your *property!* You can keep me locked away forever if you want, can't you?"

"Yes." His voice was dangerously low. "You *are* my property. I'll keep you where I want, for however long I want, because I *own* you."

"I hate you!" I shouted, my body shaking with rage.

He laughed. "You keep telling yourself that." He turned and walked out of the room, closing the door behind him.

I wanted to scream, but I wouldn't give him the satisfaction, so I clenched my jaw until it hurt. I stayed in my room all night, fuming. Julian's mood swings were seriously pissing me off. First, he treats me like a slave, parading me though the house on a leash. Then he's spoiling me with expensive clothes, and we spend a week making love on his island. And now he's acting like he wants nothing to do with me! Was this my life now? I was so mad I wanted to start throwing furniture again, but the lack of steel shutters made me reluctant to break a window.

CHAPTER 27

The next night Helen woke me, telling me we were leaving. When I asked for more details, she told me I'd have to ask Julian. *Of course.* After I showered and got dressed, I left the bedroom and saw Julian standing in front of the windows with his hands clasped behind his back.

He turned when I walked into the room, his eyes moving over me. "Are you ready?"

I nodded. "Where are we going?"

"New York."

I blinked, surprised. "Why? We just got here. I thought we were going to a wedding?"

"The wedding is in New York."

I was confused. "Then why did we come to London?"

He put his hand in his pants pockets and stared at me.

"*What*?" I snapped angrily.

"I'm trying to decide how much to tell you."

I huffed. "How about everything?"

He looked at me silently for several moments before speaking. "We came to London because I only recently purchased this property, so few know about it. I thought this would be the safest place for you."

"Why were you concerned for my safety?" I asked slowly.

"There was a problem with another vampire. A rather *violent* vampire. I had to keep you safe until I took care of things."

My mind was spinning. *He had only wanted to keep me safe?* "Why didn't you tell me?"

"It would only have upset you."

I took a step towards him. "Disappearing without a word for three nights upset me. I didn't know if you were hurt, or if you'd just gotten tired of me."

He crossed the distance between us and lifted a hand to brush his fingers over my cheek. "I will never tire of you."

And just like that my anger was gone. I melted against him, lifting my face for a kiss. He lowered his head and brushed his lips across mine. Someone behind me cleared their throat, and Julian slowly lifted his head.

"The jet is waiting," Maria said.

Julian took my hand in his. "We're ready."

Maria rode with us in the limo to the airport, and Helen followed in another car with the three male vampires who'd accompanied us from Madrid.

We boarded Julain's jet and took off, and Helen and Maria disappeared into the room at the back of the plane. The three guys sat in the main cabin with us so I never got a chance to speak privately with Julian. Or to kiss him again.

"Who's getting married?" I asked, finally breaking the silence.

Julian gave me a small smile. "My younger sister, Adeline."

My eyebrows shot up. "Your younger sister?"

He chuckled. "Well, my sister, in the sense that we were both changed by the same vampire. She was changed four hundred years after me."

My eyebrows shot up. "So quite a *bit* younger." I wondered if I'd ever get used to the fact that the people around me were hundreds of years old. How would I feel when I was that old? "Tell me about the wedding," I said, to distract myself from that thought. "You said there would be a week-long celebration?"

He frowned. "Unfortunately, we've missed most of it. We'll only be there for one night, for the wedding ceremony."

I frowned. We'd missed his sister's wedding festivities because he'd spent the last four nights dealing with the bad vampire. I wish I'd gotten the chance to ask him more about that. Although he probably would have refused to tell me, and then I'd have gotten pissed and we'd have ended up in another argument. I turned to look out the window, wondering if our relationship would always be that turbulent.

I don't know what I expected. We only met a couple weeks ago. It was strange to remember that. Sometimes I felt so close to him, like I'd known him forever. Sometimes he acted like he cared about me, and other times he acted like he hated me. We're all vampires like that? Moody and temperamental? Adam hadn't been. He'd always been kind. He would never have locked me away or kept secrets from me.

Except he did. A traitorous voice in my head whispered. *He kept the biggest secret of all.*

W̲e landed at a private runway in New York and drove half an hour to the estate where the wedding was being held. It was a three-story mansion made of light-colored stone that gleamed in the moonlight. Every light in the house was on, and I could hear music before we even got out of the car.

Julian wanted to avoid the crowd, so we entered through the backdoor and took the servants' stairs up to our room. The sounds drifting upstairs from the party sounded a lot more boisterous than the ball I'd attended, and I briefly wondered if a vampire orgy was taking place. When we got to our room Julian ushered me inside and closed the door behind us, cutting off the sounds from below.

"*Well*," I said with a little laugh. "It sounds like a real party down there."

He shrugged out of his suit jacket. "You have *no* idea. Vampire weddings can get very..." He laughed and shook his head. "Let's just say it's probably a good thing we missed most of it."

I smiled suggestively. "Well now I need *all* the details."

He tossed his jacket onto a chair and walked towards me. "I've got a better idea." He unbuttoned the cuffs of his shirt and my heart sped up.

"I want to talk first." I held up a hand to stop him, even as my body began to respond to his suggestion.

"Talk?" He stopped in front of me and lowered his head to press a kiss to the side of my neck, before inhaling deeply. "I don't want to talk." He murmured, his lips moving against my skin as he spoke.

I shuddered with pleasure. I knew what he wanted, I wanted it too. But we had some things to hash out before I gave him access to my body again. I pressed my hands to his chest and half-heartedly tried to push him away. He grabbed my hips and pulled me tight against him. He kissed his way across my neck and my head fell back.

"I mean it," I breathed, as my eyes fluttered closed. One of his hands slid up my body to cup my breast and my nipples hardened instantly. He growled in response, his thumb brushing over my nipple.

"Julian," I gasped, fighting the urge to give in. "I need to know what I am to you."

His hand stilled, and he raised his head from my neck to look at me.

"What is this between us?" I asked, afraid of what his answer would be.

He looked at me for the longest time before answering. "I don't know."

"You don't know how you feel?" I tried to hide my disappointment.

He frowned slightly. "I feel very protective of you. And very possessive." His hand was still cupping my breast, and he squeezed it gently. "You *belong* to me, Sarah."

I squeezed my thighs together, hating how much his words turned me on. "I don't want to be your property." I told him, even as I pressed my breast against his hand. "And how do you know you really want me? What if it's all just a reaction to drinking my blood?"

Julian rubbed his thumb across my nipple and leaned in to kiss my neck again. "I've fed from countless vampires," he murmured against my skin, "and I've never wanted any of them the way that I want you." He slid his free hand down my body and rubbed me between the legs. "I take care of my possessions, Sarah. Let me take care of you."

My body jerked in response. "I don't want to just be your possession," I breathed, rocking my hips against his hand. He went to unfasten my pants, and I grabbed his wrists. "Julian."

He silenced me with a kiss. My body grew weak, and he took the opportunity to unfasten my pants. He slid a hand inside, going right for my pussy. I was shamelessly wet already, and he slid two fingers inside of me. I moaned into his mouth. And he nipped at my lower lip.

"Julian," I gasped, grabbing his biceps to steady myself.

"Yes," he murmured, pushing his fingers deeper. "Say my name."

I gave in to the pleasure, forgetting all about the conversation I wanted to have.

CHAPTER 28

The following night was the wedding. Helen styled my hair again, braiding it into a crown atop my head and holding it in place with diamond pins that sparkled in the light when I turned my head.

I wore a black satin gown that was fitted to the waist before flowing loosely to the ground. Even in my stilettos, the gown brushed the floor when I walked. It had a slit on one side that went all the way up to my hip bone, making undergarments impossible. It was sexy and daring, and entirely inappropriate for a wedding, but Julian insisted I wore it. He told me I'd fit right in, and if that was true, I couldn't imagine what everyone else would be wearing.

Before we went down, Julian fastened a necklace around my neck. I stood in front of the mirror and watched as he put it on me. It was a thick diamond choker, with an enormous diamond pendant hanging in the front.

He ran his hands down my bare arms and leaned down to press a kiss to my neck, just below my ear. "You look stunning," he murmured against my skin, causing a shiver to run through me. He turned me to face him and my eyes moved over him appreciatively.

He wore an all black tux, with black diamond cufflinks near-ly as big as the pendant at my throat. The black collar of his shirt against the tan skin of his throat made my mouth water. I wanted to scrape my fangs across his neck, and mark him as mine for all to see.

My nipples hardened at the thought, and his eyes fell to my chest. The satin material made my arousal far too obvious.

"The night hasn't even begun and I already want it to be over." He brushed his knuckles back and forth over one nipple as he spoke. "When we get back to this room, I'm going to taste every inch of your body."

I couldn't wait. "Promise?"

N othing could have prepared me for the wedding. The ceremony itself was held in a separate building which looked like a gothic church with no windows. Tall candelabras illuminated the space and there was a large stone altar at the front of the room that made me wonder what they used it for. The vampire who officiated the wedding was dressed in a robe and tall pointed hat that reminded me of the pope, except the material was blood red with black trim.

The bride was stunning, in a black ball gown with a long, lace train. She had the palest skin, and blonde hair so light that it reminded me of Allie. The groom was surprisingly average looking, at least as far as vampires were concerned. Julian and I were in the front row, and as the head of the family he had to step forward to give his official consent.

Instead of exchanging rings and making vows, the bride and groom cut their wrists with a gold dagger and let their blood flow into a golden chalice. Then, while the vampire pope said a bunch of stuff in a language I didn't recognize, the bride and groom took turns drinking from the cup.

After the ceremony, we all moved to the ballroom, where a few hundred more guests were waiting. I almost stopped in my tracks when I saw the size of the crowd, but Julian swept me into the room with a confidence I envied.

It wasn't long before I started to relax. With Julian at my side I felt safe, and his relaxed attitude had a calming effect on me. We mingled and danced, and before long I was having a wonderful time.

When we waltzed, Julian spun me so fast that I tossed my head back and laughed, unaware of the attention we were getting. When we mingled, he stood with his hand at the small of my back, moving his fingers in small circles, often dipping lower than was proper.

A few hours passed, and I was standing with Julian while he spoke with several other guests. I kept a pleasant smile on my face, pretending to listen while I secretly watched the room. Julian didn't seem to notice that the atmosphere was changing, but I did. The dancers were still waltzing, but it was different now. More erotic somehow. They held each other closer and spun faster. At times I could swear their feet weren't touching the floor.

People's eyes were darkening, and couples were embracing and kissing in the corners of the room. I stared at one couple, trying to decipher if the man was kissing his companion's neck or feeding, and reluctantly tore my eyes away from them when Julian said my name.

"Sarah, I'd like to introduce you to my brother Hector, and his lovely wife Olivia."

I smiled at the couple. "It's nice to meet you both."

"We've heard so much about you," Olivia said, taking my hand in hers. "I do hope we can be friends."

"I'd like that," I said, trying not to show how surprised I was by her friendliness. The vampires I'd met so far were not nearly so open with their feelings.

"Sarah." Hector bowed his head to me, and my eyes widened with surprise. Julian was usually the one they bowed to, not me.

Hector turned to Julian. "May I speak with you privately?"

Julian frowned slightly, but nodded. He looked down at me. "I'll just be a moment. Olivia will keep you company until I return." He gave Olivia a look, and when she grinned back at him he scowled playfully. "Don't cause trouble."

"I wouldn't dream of it," she said sweetly, and I decided right then that we *would* be friends.

Julian brushed his hand across my ass as he walked away and I glanced quickly at Olivia to see if she noticed. Her grin told me she had.

"So what do you think?" She asked brightly.

"About what?"

She waved a hand towards the dancers. "This. The ball. The wedding. Vampires. *Julian*?" She looked at me sideways.

I laughed. "Well, that's a loaded question."

She scrunched her nose. "Sorry. I know I'm being nosy. It's just that Julian hasn't been like this for so long. It's gotten our hopes up."

I looked at her. "Like what?"

"Happy." She turned away to watch the dancers, as if she hadn't just dropped a bomb on me, and I stared at her until she looked at me again. "Sorry," she said again. "I shouldn't have said anything. But you're happy, right? With Julian?" When I didn't answer she continued. "Because you sure *seem* happy."

I suddenly wanted to confide in her. To pour my heart out and tell her everything I'd been through. Instead, I only nodded. "Yes. I'm happy."

She looked relieved when I said it. "I'm so glad." She linked her arm through mine. "Now," she said, turning to face the crowd again. "Let's see what kind of trouble we can get into."

Olivia led me through the room, pointing out people and filling my ear with juicy gossip, and before long we were laughing like old friends. After a while, the groom approached and told Olivia the bride needed her. Olivia made me promise to remain where I was before leaving. I stood where she left me, near some open French doors leading out onto a balcony, until a familiar scent drifted in on a breeze. *Julian was outside.*

Thinking this would be the perfect opportunity for a moonlit kiss, I ducked outside. The night air felt so wonderful after being in the crowded ballroom, that I briefly wondered why vampires didn't hold their parties outdoors. Then I heard Julian's voice.

I stepped to the balcony rail and looked down. Below me was a wide stone patio with stairs leading down into a garden. I could hear Julian and Hector talking, but I couldn't see where they were. I was just about to call out to them, when Hector's words stopped me.

"So Adam escaped again."

I froze, not even daring to breathe.

"Yes." I heard Julian say. "Whoever is helping him seems to have endless resources."

My heart began to pound, beating louder and louder until it was all I could hear. It drowned out Julian's words and the sounds of the party. *Adam was alive.* I was still standing there when Julian found me. He took one look at me and knew that I'd heard him.

Before I even had time to speak he grabbed me in his arms and flew us both up over the house. We came down in a court-yard on the other side, far from the ballroom. As soon as my feet hit the ground, I shoved him with all my strength. He stumbled backwards several feet, but did not fall.

"Adam is alive!" I shouted, pressing my hands to the sides of my head.

Julian's expression was unreadable. "Yes."

"How?"

"Someone helped him escape."

My blood was pumping so fast I felt dizzy. "Where is he?"

"I don't know."

I shook my head. "I don't understand! You said he was going to be executed the night we left! When did he escape? How are we just now finding out?" I looked at him with wild eyes and his expression told me everything. "You already knew." My voice was barely a whisper.

He stepped towards me, holding out his hand. "This changes nothing between us."

"This changes everything!" I screamed. I tore the choker off my neck and threw it at him. "When did you find out?" I shouted the question at him. "*When?*"

He let his hand fall to his side. "It doesn't matter when."

"How could you keep this from me?" I cried, my voice breaking.

"Telling you would have only caused you more pain," he said, stepping closer. "Adam escaped, but when they find him again he'll be executed. They will find him, Sarah."

"When?" I asked again. "When did you know?"

Julian straightened. "When we returned home from the island."

I stared at him, too stunned to speak. Then a realization hit me. "That's why we went to London. You hid me away because Adam escaped. You didn't want him to find me."

"Yes."

Oh my god! I felt like I was going to hyperventilate. "Did you go looking for him? Is that why you disappeared?" Then I remembered how messed up he'd looked when he returned. "Did you find him?"

"I don't know where he is. I swear it."

I blinked furiously, trying to hold back my tears. "I don't believe you."

"I never lie, Sarah."

"Everything you've done has been a lie!" I shrieked. "You kept this from me! Last night- Last night, when we made love you knew Adam was alive! You kept it from me so I'd stay with you! You only wanted me as part of your sick revenge against him!" I shoved him, and he stumbled backwards before steadying himself. "You never wanted *me*! You only wanted to hurt *him*!" I shoved him again. "The only time you've ever been honest was when you put that fucking collar on me and paraded me down to Adam's cell!" I tried to shove him again, but he grabbed my arms and yanked me against him.

He leaned over me until our faces almost touched. "I *never* lied to you," he snarled. "When we were on the island, I thought Adam was dead. There were no tricks. Everything that happened between us was real." He shook me for emphasis. "I was told the night we returned to Madrid, and I didn't tell you because it changes nothing between us. Adam is the one who lied to you. He took your life, and continued to keep that from you, even after he fucked you!"

I surged forward with my fangs bared, intending to tear his throat out, but he jerked away. He released me and stepped back. He stared at me, his expression unreadable, and I glared back, my chest heaving with every breath. I wanted to kill him, but I also wanted to lay my head on his chest and cry.

"Go to the room," he finally said. "We're leaving tomorrow. I'll come for you when it's time to go."

"So that's it?" I asked, with disbelief. "We're just supposed to go on like nothing's changed?"

"Nothing *has* changed." His hands fisted at his sides. "You still belong to me."

I spun away from him and ran into the house. I ran all the way to the bedroom, encountering no one besides a couple of surprised servants. I flung the bedroom door open and slammed it shut behind me. I felt so consumed by my anger that I squeezed my eyes shut and screamed.

"Sarah."

My eyes flew open, and there he was. *Adam.*

CHAPTER 29

With a sob I flung myself at him, and he caught me in his arms.

"It's okay," he whispered, stroking my hair. "You're okay now. I've got you."

Tears ran down by face, but for once I didn't care. "Oh my god!" I cried, squeezing him tightly.

He gently pulled away. "We have to leave. Now." I nodded and wiped at my tears. "I have friends waiting, who'll help us." He took me by the hand. "We'll go out the window and I'll fly us off the property. There's a car waiting for us out on the main road."

Adam pulled me towards the window, and for a moment I let him. I'd been so angry with Julian, and so relieved to see Adam alive, I momentarily forgot about all the secrets and lies. But as I stepped towards the window, it all came crashing back to me.

I dug my heels into the carpet, pulling us both to a stop. "You changed me."

He tugged on my hand, glancing nervously towards the door. "We have to hurry."

I yanked my hand free. "You changed me, didn't you?"

"Sarah!" His expression was panicked. "We have to go now, we can talk when we get to the car!"

I shook my head. "I'm not going anywhere until you tell me the truth. About everything."

He reached for my hand again, but I stepped away. He looked at me with wild eyes. "There's no time for this! We have to go!" He looked at the door again.

"Tell me!" I shouted.

"Shhhh!" He looked at the door, we both did, waiting for someone to come bursting through. When no one appeared, he shoved his hands through his hair. "What do you want me to say? You already know the truth."

A lump formed in my throat, but I refused to shed any more tears for him. "Why?" I asked, my voice breaking. "Why did you do this to me?"

"Because I loved you."

I grew still. *He loved me?*

He took a deep, shuddering breath. "I was turned against my will, by one of the oldest vampires, Valentina Velasco. I hated her for it. I tried to kill her, but she was so much stronger. I tried to run away, but she caught me and dragged me back. She wanted me to worship her like the others did, but I refused. I begged her to let me go. I told her I was engaged to a woman I loved, but that was the worst thing I could have said. She starved me for three nights, then brought in my fiance. I tore her to pieces, and Valentina watched, laughing. She'd starve me until I was out of my mind, then she'd feed me her blood.

When I was high on her venom, she fucked me. Can you imagine how I felt when I came down from that high?"

Adam looked at me with such anguish, that my heart broke for him. He glanced at the door again before continuing. "I tried to end my life by going out in the sun, but she sent day-walkers after me. They healed me completely, then whipped my back until my skin hung in ribbons. They starved me for weeks so my wounds wouldn't heal. After that she kept me chained during daylight hours. Usually in her bedchamber.

"Eventually one of the others took pity on me and agreed to help me escape. They unchained me so I could run, but I didn't run. Not until after I killed her. I knew Julian would hunt me for the rest of my existence. Hiding was easy in the beginning. But with the technological advances over the years, security cameras and cell phones, the only way to remain hidden was to live as a recluse. For the last sixty years I've been completely alone. Sometimes I'd luck out and find an abandoned house to live in for a while, but more often than not I lived in the woods, like an animal.

"I was losing my last shred of humanity. Whenever I encountered a lone hiker in the woods, I killed them without remorse. I was becoming a monster, like Valentina. So I decided to end it." Adam smiled coldly. "But I was going out with a bang. I was going to walk into the middle of the city, where a hundred cameras would be pointed at me, and take out as many humans as possible. I was going to bathe the streets in blood. Cause a scene that would prove to the world that vampires existed. What would the police think when they emptied their guns into me, and still I stood? Eventually, the Strategoi would find me and kill me. And I'd finally be free."

Adam stared at me, his expression eerily blank. I couldn't believe what he'd told me. The Adam I knew seemed like a completely different person from the one he described. I'd never be able to comprehend the depths of his pain, after everything he'd been through, but was he really planning on massacring a bunch of humans?

"But things didn't go as planned," he continued, smiling sadly. "When I walked into the center of town that night, I saw you. You were playing your violin, and for some reason I decided to wait. To listen for *just* a moment. Only I ended up listening all night. I followed you home, confused by how easily you'd distracted me from my plans. There was something about you…"

He stepped closer to me and lifted a hand to tuck a strand of hair behind my ear. I remained still, allowing him, and he cupped my cheek with his hand. "I returned the following night, and the night after that. The way you played your violin…" He paused, as if searching for the right words. "It was like you were playing just for me. Your song called to the darkness in me, and I knew you were meant to be mine. Slowly, I felt my humanity returning. I began to feed without killing again. I followed you home every night to make sure you were safe, and when you were attacked, I was there. I pulled him off you and snapped his neck. I flew his body out of the city and dumped it, before returning to you. I sat on your fire escape and listened to you cry, and your pain made me want to burn the city to the ground."

"You were there?" I asked, my voice thick with emotion.

He nodded. "I followed you to your sister's house. I was there, when you stood in the field. I heard your plea, Sarah. You said you couldn't handle it anymore. You needed it to be over. You had a hard, thankless job, a rundown apartment, no money, no hope, no joy. I thought I could give you a better life. And yes, I wanted to be with you. I loved you already."

I was stunned. "You loved me? Before ever even talking to me?"

"Yes. And I love you still. And I know you love me too."

"I don't know what I feel!" I cried, pulling away from him. "How can I know its real, and not just a reaction to your venom?"

Adam lifted his hand, then let it fall. "I don't know. But I know what *I* feel is real. I've fed from many vampires, and I've never felt this way before."

I laughed harshly. "That's exactly what Julian said. I think you're both full of shit!"

Adam went still, and his eyes filled with fury. "Julian told you he loves you?"

I swallowed, feeling afraid of Adam for the first time. "Not exactly."

His eyes darkened until no white showed. "What did he say?" He stepped closer. "What did he *do*?

"I-"

The door burst open, flying off its hinges, as Julian flew into the room. He slammed into Adam, flying across the room with him, slamming him in the far wall.

"Julian!" I screamed, scrambling out of the way.

Adam roared and shoved off the wall, taking Julian with him. They flew across the room and slammed into the other wall, cracking the plaster.

"Stop!" I shrieked. But they would never stop. This was a fight centuries in the making. I backed away until I bumped into the wall.

They fought like animals, with their claws and teeth. They moved so fast it was hard for my eyes to follow. It was terrifying. Even more terrifying was the fact that I didn't know who I wanted to win.

They went crashing through the door into the bathroom, and I saw my chance. I ran. Down the stairs, and back out into the courtyard where Julian and I had just argued. I never slowed to see if any guards were nearby. I bolted across the courtyard, across the lawn, and into the treeline. Still, I didn't stop. Not even when my instincts told me that the dawn was approaching. Not until I saw the sky began to lighten.

I finally stumbled to a stop and leaned heavily against a tree. I was gasping for air, and my dress was in shreds. I had no idea how far I'd run. I'd never once even slowed down to listen, to see if anyone followed.

I forced myself to breathe quietly, but all I heard was the morning chorus of the birds in the trees. I strained my ears, but

I was alone. I was alone in the woods, and the sun was coming up.

I pushed off the tree and started to jog, my eyes darting from side to side, looking for shelter, but finding none. *Was this the end for me?*

Soft rays of light were beginning to fall through the leaves overhead. I quickened my pace, fighting the panic that threatened to overtake me. I needed to stay calm, and focus. A sob escaped me, the sound echoing in my ears. Then there was another sound. A dog's bark.

I skidded to a halt, tilting my head from side to side as I strained my ears. I heard it again, and my head snapped to the side, looking in that direction. Where there were dogs there were people, and where there were people there was shelter.

I ran towards the sound, not knowing what I'd do when I reached my destination. I slowed when I saw light ahead. The trees had thinned, and I could see an open area ahead. And a house. I froze, all of my senses suddenly kicking into overdrive.

The dog barked again, then someone whistled. "Come on, Sunny!" A woman called. The dog barked again, and a few moments later I heard a car door shut. I crept forward slowly. I was approaching the back of the house and couldn't see the woman or the dog.

I heard the engine turn on, then saw the car appear. It drove down the driveway, away from the house. I remained where I was for several minutes after it disappeared from sight, listening for any sounds that would indicate there was still someone home. On the far side of the house, the first rays of sun peeked over the trees, and I knew I had to act.

I ran towards the house at full speed. My skin began to burn as I tore across the back lawn, and when I jumped up onto the back porch, I was gasping in pain. I threw open the door, thanking god it was unlocked, and shut it behind me. I froze, listening, but the house was empty.

I moved quickly, looking for a place to hide until nightfall. I searched for a basement door, but there was none. Finally, I went upstairs into what appeared to be an unused guestroom. I stepped into the small closet and closed the door. Several winter coats were hanging in there, and I pulled them down, stuffing them against the crack at the bottom of the door. Satisfied that no sunlight would make its way in, I sat on the floor and leaned back against the wall.

The closet was too small for me to stretch out my legs, so I bent them in front of me and wrapped my arms around them. That's when I realized I was barefoot. I blinked, surprised. When had I lost my shoes? I leaned my head forward against my knees and forced myself to think.

I thought about the fight, remembering how Adam and Julian tore into each other. I'd been sure they were going to kill each other, and maybe they had. Maybe one of them was dead now. *But who?* And what happened when the survivor realized I was gone? Did they chase after me? Did I want them to? And what would I do when night came? I couldn't keep running forever, I needed a plan. But the sun was now up, and I could fight sleep no longer.

I woke with a start, my body tense, my senses instantly alert. I could hear sounds from below. A woman was talking, but the conversation was one-sided, so I knew she was on the phone. I could smell food cooking, so I assumed she was in the kitchen. I'd come in through the kitchen this morning, so I'd have to find a different way out.

I pulled the coats away from the door, and no light came in. I slowly cracked the door open and saw the room was dark. Night had fallen. I stood and pushed the door open, then I glanced down at my shredded gown. I needed clothes.

Only coats hung in the closet, so I grabbed the longest one, a puffer jacket that hung almost to my knees. I shrugged into it, then paused to listen again. Not knowing where the dog was, I was hesitant to go downstairs.

I went to the window and unlocked it before sliding it open. I pushed myself through, landing silently on the grass below, my body tucking into a crouched position. I waited a moment, listening, then I bolted across the front lawn and the driveway, into the woods on the opposite side.

I ran all night. I kept to the woods as much as possible, but at times I was forced to cross roads or open fields. I fed off a deer I encountered, and hid in a shed when dawn approached. I curled up in a ball between the wall and a riding lawn mower and prayed the rickety building would keep out the sun.

The following night, as I ran, I began to recognize my surroundings. I was getting close. I stopped after a while, knowing

I needed to feed before facing my sister. I killed a cow, feeling guilty about killing a domesticated animal, but it was better than killing a human.

When I reached our back field, I slowed to a walk. My heart was hammering. *Was I making the right choice?*

It was the middle of the night when I approached the house, but Allie was sitting on the back porch, wrapped in a blanket. With my vampire sight, I could see her long before she saw me, and I stared at her face as I approached, taking in every beautiful detail.

When I reached the back lawn, I knew she saw me. I saw her eyes focus on me and heard her heartbeat speed up. She stood up slowly, letting the blanket fall. The wind carried her scent to me and I wanted to weep. I was home.

The Story Continues...

Who won the fight between Julian and Adam, and what did the victor do when he realized Sarah was gone? To find out, order your copy of *The Darkest Crown*. Follow Sarah as she is pulled deeper into the world of vampires, where magic and madness go hand, and love is a force so powerful not even death can stop it.

AUTHOR'S NOTE

Thank you for reading *The Darkest Song*. If you enjoyed it (I hope you did!) please consider leaving a review on Amazon. As a new indie author, reviews are so very important.

Now a little bit about me... For as long as I can remember I've been obsessed with magic and fantasy. When I was young I looked for fairies under mushrooms, and made "magical potions" out of dandelions and moss, and whatever else I found growing in my backyard. Then I watched *Bram Stoker's Dracula*, and my fascination took a darker turn. *Vampires*. Immortal, powerful, and passionate. Their love was all-consuming, and everlasting. *And I wanted it.*

That was the beginning of my writing career. I filled my diary with short stories about hot vampires, which eventually led to stories about hot fae and hot gods (I didn't get into aliens until much later, but believe me, they were worth the wait). So if you enjoyed *The Darkest Song*, strap in and hold on. I've got 20 years of smutty fantasies coming your way!

I love hearing from readers! Visit AmyAtley.com and sign up for my newsletter for all the latest book news, bonus content, and more!

Printed in Dunstable, United Kingdom

65243658R00140